Halloween Jack

and the
Devil's Gate

By:

M. Todd Gallowglas

For Trey, Steve, and Snipe
Thanks for years of encouragement

Acknowledgements

First and foremost, I want to thank Robin, the wonderful lady for believing enough in my dreams to not let me quit even when I felt like throwing in the towel. Alex Jimenez, where ever he is for teaching me the "Jack of the Lantern" story. Marti and Bill for giving me a shot at this whole storytelling thing. All the folks at De Vere's pub in Sacramento; I couldn't ask for a better place to start my professional writing career. The wonderful ladies who work the morning shift at Starbucks in Lincoln, CA for pouring me coffee and dealing with my anguished cries as I finished this manuscript.

And again, Mathew and Robert for giving me the greatest stories I can ever tell.

Books by M. Todd Gallowglas:

The TEARS OF RAGE Sequence
First Chosen
Once We Were Like Wolves
Arms of the Storm
Judge of Dooms
The Fires of Night *

Jaludin's Road

Halloween Jack and the Curse of Frost
Halloween Jack and the Red Emperor *

The Dragon Bone Flute
Legacy of the Dragon Bone Flute *

* Forthcoming.

Table of Contents:

Halloween Jack

Prologue

It started with a turnip. True, some stories say it was a gourd, others go with the now traditional pumpkin, but, in truth, that first lantern John the blacksmith carved was out of a turnip. That's when he first became known as Jack of the Lantern. The stories don't all agree on how it was that Jack made the Devil so angry that the Devil wouldn't let Jack into Hell, but the fact remains that all humanity owes Jack a debt, for as time went on and the Devil and his kin became free to roam the world only one night of the year, we carve our turnips, gourds, and pumpkins into lanterns to put outside our doors. We know, that the Devil and his kin know, behind one of those lanterns is a troublemaker of the likes they can do without.

However, deep in the bowels of his dark realm, sitting on his dark throne, the Dark One has not forgotten. While Jack of the Lantern has wandered over the centuries, the Devil and his kin, cunning and crafty one and all, have plotted and schemed their revenge.

One

Moira O'Neil went about the cottage as she did every Halloween, serving the demons that came through the cottage. While she did, Grandmother checked the demons off the list, one by one, as they returned from their once-a-year excursion into the world of men. Though there were plenty of chairs in the cottage, the demons all stood. With good reason, the demons did not trust the chairs in this house.

One of the demons said something unflattering in Latin to Moira as she plopped a lump of sugar into its tea. It was a tiny little runt of an imp, green and yellow skin, with tiny little horns barely poking out of its forehead, though it did have a long tail that Moira kept having to step around. Just because they were demons didn't mean Grandmother would tolerate her being a poor hostess. Stepping on tails was among the first signs of a poor hostess.

"Oh, right," Moira said, and switched the cup with the demon sitting next to the imp. That was a succubus, with barely enough clothing on to force a man's imagination. "Apologies, Miss Saleesh."

Moira knew the succubus's name because this particular temptress had come out on Halloween every year since Moira could remember.

"Not at all, dear," Saleesh said. "It's been a long night for all of us."

Moira spat in the cup she placed in front of the imp. "Happy now then?"

The imp gave a curt nod and began to sip daintily at his tea.

"Best hurry with your refreshments," Grandmother's deep Irish voice came from over by the door. "Dawn's close, she is. Don't want to be caught behind. Recall what happen last year? Himself will be along any moment to take note of the stragglers."

Most of the demons grumbled in agreement, even the most brazen of them. The man they called The Lantern came just before dawn, on the off chance that one of the demons tried to stay in the human world beyond sunrise.

"Now I'm not normally one to bless anything," Moira heard one of the demons say in a very proper British accent as she handed him a glass of wine, "but I have to say I'm quite pleased with this rise of science and Natural Philosophy. People are forgetting the traditions, and I was able to collect three very impressive souls this year."

"Three?" his companion remarked. "And I thought I was doing quite well with one. Might I accompany you next year? I must know how you do it?"

"But of course. The more we share, the better we're served."

Over the last few years, Moira had heard demons bragging more and more about successes in soul collecting. And they all ascribed it to finding mortals that weren't protecting themselves on Halloween, or as the demons called it, the Darkest Night. Normally, one had to be careful of the things one believed that came from the mouths of demons, as their kind were crafty, cunning, conniving, malicious, malevolent, and most other unpleasant adjectives one might ascribe to them. However, demons were usually truthful with each other over matters of soul collecting. Yes, they were deceitful, but they were also proud and despised being caught in a lie.

As much as Moira wished she could do something about it, she could not. The bargain made by her penultimate grandmother forbade any of the daughters in this line of Jack's blood from interfering with demons on this night so that these daughters could protect humanity the other three hundred sixty-four nights of the year – sixty-five on leap years.

Serving a mug of beer to a hulking monstrosity of all tentacles and claws, Moira felt something brush at the hairs that had come loose from her bun. Faster than anyone might think possible, she pulled a switch out of her apron ties and snapped it across the forearm of a goblin hanging by its tail from the rafters. The sickly looking, greenish-gray creature strung together a slew of insults from at least a dozen languages. Its skin bubbled and burned where the silver crosses imbedded in the switch struck its skin. Other demons, the older ones who had been through the gate many times on the Darkest Night, laughed and howled.

"They knows us better 'n tha'," called a creature that looked human except for the hooves, curling horns, and goat-like eyes. That one was a duke of Hell at least, perhaps even a prince.

Moira curtsied to the demon and went about her serving.

The goblin had been reaching for her locket, which contained a strand of hair from Saint Mary, one of the seven items needed to perform the ritual that kept the Devil's Gate closed the rest of the year. Every year, as the Darkest Night came to a close, some of the demons tried to steal an item or two, but they always failed. Grandmother had taught Moira to mind them well. And as sneaky as they sometimes were, after a while demons became rather predictable. At sixteen, Moira felt that while she didn't know everything about them, she knew enough to expect their tricks.

Moira stifled a yawn as she collected used cups and glasses. She timed each night by her yawns. This was her third this evening. The cottage seemed a bit more crowded this year than normal by her third yawn, and there seemed quite a few demons she didn't recognize. The list of demons who were allowed to roam cycled every couple of years, and it took a lot for demons to get on the list to wander the world on the darkest night. Moira glanced at the great grandfather clock on the far side of the room, the one that showed not the hours of the day, but the balance between night and day. Dawn was almost upon them.

As she cleaned up after the demons, who were definitely *not* leaving as usual when they finished their drinks, Moira made her way over to Grandmother. One look in Grandmother's eyes told Moira that Grandmother had noticed it too.

The clock chimed ten minutes to dawn. Moira glanced at the list in Grandmother's hand. So many demons hadn't checked in yet.

The door opened and six demons came in, imps and goblins all. The last two had tails wrapped around their arms so as not to get them trapped in the door.

"Is it too late for refreshments?" one of them asked.

"Only if you take what you get without complaining," Grandmother said. "You don't have time for special orders at this late hour."

"Thank you kindly," they all said, bobbing their heads.

Moira poured them all tea and spat into the ones she gave the imps.

A minute later, a pair of spiny things came in, and Grandmother told them they were too late and to start making their way to the gate.

At five minutes to dawn, the cottage was more crowded than Moira had ever seen it. It was also hotter than it had ever been before. Her dirty blond hair clung to her face.

"Alrighty then," Grandmother spoke up. "I do not ken what you all think you're waiting on, but best be getting home."

At that moment, the door bust open. A demon with blue skin, with its shoulders up around its ears and twin scorpion stingers twitching behind its back, rushed in. The creature's eyes were wide, and its mouth opened and closed as it tried to form words. Finally its mind seemed to catch up to what it wanted to say.

"He's coming." Those first two words came out barely above a hoarse whisper. Then the scorpion demon spoke louder. "Listen to me! He's almost here! The Lantern is coming!"

Silence crashed down on the cottage like a physical weight. It seemed as if, all at once, every demon in the cottage gave a slow, nervous swallow.

Then the stampede began.

Now, Moira had never seen a stampede, having never been to the A-merican Colonies, but her penultimate grandfather brought her adventure books from all across the world. She loved reading about the American West, and if she were ever going to see anything that ever resembled a stampede, this mass retreat of demons would definitely qualify. Screaming, stamping, and crashing furniture filled the space previously occupied by the silence.

In a moment, silence descended again, this time with a noticeable absence of demons. Moira went to shut the back door before putting on a fresh pot of tea for her penultimate grandfather. Only, the cottage wasn't completely empty. One little imp remained, standing in the middle of the room and facing the front door of the cottage. The creature's head came up to Moira's waist. It had blood red skin, and its eyes glowed like embers in a dying fire. It wore the trousers, waistcoat, and frock coat of a gentleman. One of its horns curled up and back behind its floppy ear, but the other had been broken off only a few inches above the imp's forehead. The stump was rounded, indicating the injury had come some time ago.

"Better get yourself out," Grandmother said, making a shooing motion with her hand. "Things may get bad if you stay."

"Shut it, you old hag," the imp said. "I've got some words for Mr. Jack of the Lantern. It's been a long time coming. I'll speak my mind and be off on my merry way once I'm done."

"Fine," Grandmother replied. "Your funeral."

The imp spat. "No funeral for demons. Much as we could wish it otherwise on occasion, we can't die. But even if we did, where would we go?"

The three of them waited, the silence broken only by the chime of the clock each minute closer to sunrise: three minutes, two minutes, one minute.

The clock gave a massive *GONG* as dawn came. At that moment the door swung open. The imp began to shake, though Moira couldn't tell if it was in anger or terror – perhaps an equal combination of both. A form filled the doorway, not from size, but from the pure potency of his legend. Were they truly in the real world, the man would have only been short and stocky, looking so much like the blacksmith he'd been before he took up the lantern. But the cottage stood in one of the in-between-places where worlds touched and legends and myths took on their own realities, at the border between all places.

Jack of the Lantern stood in the doorway, framed by dawn's light as he always was on the dawn after the Darkest Night. His coat, once fine, now hung mostly ragged which only served to enhance his terrible visage. In his left hand, Jack held a lantern, carved from a turnip this year. The face of it had a sad frown, and Jack had carved what seemed tears under the eyes. The flames of three candles flickered behind that frown and the eyes and tears. This lantern, and all the others he had carved from turnips, gourds, and other plants, was his namesake; this was what the Devil and all of his kin feared; this was the gift Jack had given the world to protect humanity from the goblins, imps, ghouls, and other creatures of the dark realms that were free to roam the world on All Hallow's Eve.

Moira glanced at where the little red imp stood, expecting the thing to have fled once Jack appeared. To her surprise the imp stood his ground.

"I know you," Jack said. "It's been centuries, but I know you."

"And I know you also, blacksmith," the imp said. "How could I forget you? Come to the gates when I was a watching and send me off to tell His Darkness."

"You've grown rather cheeky," Jack replied. "I'm impressed. Most of your kind doesn't want to have anything to do with me."

"That's because you still scare them. You hold no terror for me. Do you have any idea the torments I suffered just for telling His Darkness that you were at the gates? Now it's your turn to learn what centuries of torment feels like, Mr. I-Can-Not-Die."

The imp reached underneath its frock coat and pulled out a strange device about the size of a breadbasket. Steam blew out of several vents here and there, and twin metal bars protruded from the top with tiny lightning bolts arching between them. The imp pulled on a lever and twisted a dial.

The roof above them groaned and creaked. As Jack rushed forward, something pulled the roof off the cottage. Shingles and boards rained down. One struck Jack's leg, and he stumbled. Something struck Moira's shoulder. She cried out and scrambled to the wall, hoping that it might give some protection.

Cackles of laughter rang out from above. Moira looked up. Peering down upon them from the top of the wall were all the demons that she had been serving. Above them, a huge metal form flung the cottage's roof away. The monstrosity looked like a giant metal statue of a demon, except it was moving. Just like with the breadbox device, steam blew from vents and lightning crackled here and there about the thing. Its hand came down, surprisingly fast for something so large, and slammed a cage down around Jack.

The moment he was trapped, the demons invaded the cottage. Even before the first dropped down next to her, Moira had her switch in hand and was lashing out around her. Of all the relics used for the ritual, the one she wore around her neck was the only one that could not be re-placed. The others would be difficult, but it could be done. She had to e-scape with the locket.

A demon screamed as Moira slashed its face with the switch. She didn't try for the door. They'd be waiting for that, but she might have a

chance at the window. Thankfully most of the demons seemed more in-
clined to destroy the cottage and find the other ritual objects than catch
and torment Moira. She tried to ignore Grandmother's scream, but Moira's heart beat a bit faster when the cry died out.

The door blew inward. Moira was glad that she hadn't tried that. A
smaller version of the metal demon overhead entered the cottage. Moira
could see others behind it, marching toward them. How many were there?
She wanted to scream, cry, and then maybe scream some more, but the
years of her grandmother's teachings would not allow her any thought but
escape, even if it looked as if escape were impossible.

"Moira," a voice cried from above. "I give this coat, these boots, and
my chair to you freely as a child of my bloodline."

She glanced up. Jack had his arms stretched out of the cage. He held a
bundle, and seeing her looking up, he dropped it. As the bundle fell, demons scattered well away from where it might land. Moira ducked,
weaved, and switched her way toward the bundle.

Just as she reached it, a hand closed on her shoulder. She slapped the
hand with the switch. When the hand released her Moira dropped the
switch, grabbed the bundle, and spun around, unfurling Jack's ragged
coat. She caught a demon in the face with it. Where the coat touched the
demon, the material clung to the creature.

"No! Please no!" came a muffled cry from behind the cloth.

Moira twisted, wrapping the coat around her arm and shoulder. Then
dropping, she pulled the demon off its feet. She smiled at the crunching
sound it made on impact and grinned at the cry of pain that came after.

"You've my leave to let go of my coat," Moira said.

The coat pulled free of the demon's face, and Moira rolled away from
the creature. As she did, she noticed a pair of boots lying where the coat
had landed. She scurried over to them before any of the demons saw
them and realized what they were. Only the fear of the coat had kept the
boots unnoticed for so long.

When Moira reached the boots, she whipped the coat around her,
sending demons scrambling away. Then she sat next to the boots, bringing the coat over her, huddling underneath it, leaving no part of herself
exposed. She prayed as she removed her shoes and slid Jack's boots on.
Her prayers that the demons feared the power of the coat nearly as much
as they feared Jack seemed to be answered. She got the boots on, and they
hugged her feet, fitting perfectly.

Moira stood, letting the coat hang about her form. Demons surrounded her in a tight circle. They snarled, hissed, and growled at her, but
not a single one reached for her.

"Well now," Moira said. "It seems you all weren't as clever as you
thought."

A massive grinding of metal groaned behind the cottage, followed by two booming crashes. The gate had come down. After centuries upon centuries of standing and holding back the hordes of darkness, the Devil's Gate was open for any and all of Hell's creatures to roam free, and with Jack of the Lantern trapped in the cage above, no amount of carved lanterns would protect humanity from them. Luckily, men and angels with far more cunning and sense than Moira possessed had foreseen this, and they'd made preparations. Granted, she never imagined that she would be the one who would have to deal with this particular situation.

The next moment, the world seemed a few shades darker, despite the rising sun. Her skin crawled as if something had just walked over her grave. All the demons turned toward the back of the cottage and prostrated themselves. Moira realized that it wasn't walking over her grave, the something was walking toward the moment when it would put her in her grave.

"Jack's chair," she said, and clicked her heels together.

The magic of the boots carried her over the horde, planting her next to a plain wooden chair.

"Stop her, you fools!" The voice boomed over the landscape and inside Moira's head.

The horde leapt up and surged for where she'd been standing a moment before. Lying face down on the floor, they'd not seen her move. That might give her the precious seconds she needed.

Next to her, a demon noticed her and slashed its claws at her face. Moira leaned back and whipped the edge of the coat at it. The fabric barely touched the thing, but it was enough. She gripped the coat hard and pulled harder. The demon, a four-armed thing with sickly green skin and a mouth full of fangs, stumbled forward and fell into the chair.

"You've my leave to let go of the coat," Moira said, and the coat came away from the demon's hand. However, the thing struggled against the chair and couldn't get up.

Moira gripped the back of the chair. She had no idea if her plan would work, if the magic of the boots would carry the chair and the demon or if the demon's weight would pull the chair from her grip. But it was worth trying.

"My jewelry box." She clicked her heels together.

Again, the boots carried Moira into the air. The chair and the demon came with her. As they flew over a crowd of demons tearing through Grandmother's hope chest, Moira leaned down to the struggling demon's ear, or at least where its ear would have been had the thing been human.

"You've my leave to get out of the chair," Moira said.

Freed from the chair's magic, the demon slid off the seat of the chair and crashed into its fellows, taking them to the floor in a tangled mess.

Moira landed next to the fireplace. As she snatched up her jewelry box off the mantle, the back door of the cottage creaked open. Odd that it had never made that ominous sound ever before, but then, the master of all demons had never opened it before. Moira tried to keep from looking, to shut her eyes and think of where to go next.

"Good morning, Miss O'Neil," said a voice of pure sweetness and honey.

She couldn't help it. It was rude not to look at someone when they addressed you in a proper way. For all the years she'd spent with Grandmother, propriety had been one of their defenses against the demons. Now, those good manners served to be her undoing. She looked at the newcomer.

He was handsome, with slick black hair, thin mustache, and a pointed beard. He wore a scarlet tailcoat over a midnight-black waistcoat. His eyes held a mischievous twinkle, and a knowing smirk played across his lips. His appearance was almost enough to make Moira fall in love with him — he looked so perfectly the dashing and handsome male. But as it always was in the stories Jack of the Lantern had told her, where this man's feet should have been were a pair of cloven hooves. Moira kept sight of those hooves as she willed herself to speak.

"The nearest holy ground," Moira said through clenched teeth, and clicked her heels together.

As she flew away from the cottage, the demons, the massive metal thing that held Jack of the Lantern trapped, and the Dark One himself fell away. In the fields beyond the cottage, Moira saw dozens of the smaller metal things, all of them marching on the remains of the cottage as if they were knights assaulting a castle. She didn't know what to make of them, only that the Devil and his kin were free to roam the earth at will, and not one single person would be safe behind a lantern.

* * *

A short time later, Moira landed in front of the church. She burst in and placed the chair just to the left of the door. She closed the door with her foot and turned to head to the secret room in the back, almost tumbling into father McDermott as she did. The stern but kindly old priest grabbed her by the shoulders.

"What's going on?" he asked. In his panic, his brogue slipped in past his normally well-polished accent.

"The Devil's Gate came down," Moira said. "And the Dark One has Jack of the Lantern trapped by some metal creature."

15

She tried to wriggle out of Father McDermott's grip but couldn't. She saw him trying to let go of her, and then she remembered what she was wearing.

"You've leave to let go of my coat."

As she said those words, Father McDermott's hands came away. His face went as slack as his arms as he realized what this meant.

Without speaking further, they rushed to the secret room at the back of the church. The back wall of that room held shelf upon shelf of candles. Normally, these candles always burned bright and never ran out of wax. A name and a location were engraved on each candlestick. These flames represented the descendants of Jack of the Lantern.

One by one, the candles went out. As Moira and Father McDermott watched, the room went from being as bright as noon on a cloudless day to nearly black as midnight. Only three Candles remained: Moira O'Brien: St Matthew's Parish, Daniel McRory: the smithy, and John O'Brian: Boston.

"Lord in Heaven, preserve us," Father McDermott said in a hushed whisper.

"Better yet," Moira said, "preserve John and Daniel. If the demons find either one of them, we're all doomed."

"Well then, we have no time to waste," the Father said. "Did you bring your last coin?"

Two

John O'Brien huddled in the doorway of a bakery, holding a penny in one hand and the last gold coin of his family's fortune in the other. Snow had come early to Boston, and warmth from the ovens seeped through the door. The owner didn't mind folks standing there when the bakery wasn't open, but woe to anyone who tried to stand there during business hours. Her brother was a constable and made sure on a regular basis his sister's business was not suffering due to any sort of lowlife.

John heard a bit of shuffling behind him. He slid the gold coin into his fingerless glove and shoved that into the pocket of his coat. The coat wasn't as fine as it had been, but still the garment served its purpose and was not so worn that people refused him service when he managed to earn a bit of money by doing odd jobs no one else wanted. John was strong, able, and not anywhere near a fool. He should have been able to find work. However, no matter how hard he tried, he couldn't quite get the last of his Irish accent out of his mouth. The instant most *proper* folk heard it, they turned him away.

" 'Elp a poor soul on this cold night?" a voice asked.

John glanced back, mostly at the strangeness of hearing the Cockney accent in Boston.

The beggar was dressed more in rags and tatters than he was in clothes. Didn't have proper shoes, but rather strips of dirty wool wrapped around his feet. Grime and muck clung to his face to the point John wondered if any amount of scrubbing would ever get the face truly clean again.

"Spare somefink for a poor soul to get somefink warm in 'is belly?" the beggar asked.

John suppressed a sigh. Things shouldn't be this bad already. It wasn't even Halloween yet, and it was snowing as if it were close to Christmas. It had been this way every year since the British Empire had closed itself off from the world three years ago.

"Sir," John said, "come stand here, it's warm."

"Oh, fank yous," the beggar said, as he took John's place. "Right kind of yous. God and his angels bless you, young man."

"Just come and get warm," John said.

John wondered how the beggar was alive. He seemed more corpse than man, skin hanging loose on his face and fingers.

John actually sighed this time. He took his penny and placed it in the beggar's hand. The beggar's mouth opened, showing a multitude of missing teeth.

"Take this," John said. "No. Don't say a word." John raised his hand to cut the beggar off. "When the bakery opens, get yourself something warm to put in your belly."

With that, John walked away, leaving the beggar calling thanks behind him. John hoped he'd be able to find work of some kind soon. He hadn't eaten anything but broth and bread at the church in over a week.

As he walked, John tried to think of other warm places. Well, there was always St. Anthony's church, but John didn't want to rely on the church too much. The priests and sisters would never turn John away, he just had his pride. Too many people were asking for handouts, and John preferred to earn his own way in the world.

Halfway down the next block, John decided to try his luck by the docks. Sometimes sailors from several ships would make a fire in the cobbled roads near the docks and trade stories, songs, and drinks. John knew a few stories. His father had been fond of old tales of Ireland and of the early Americas, especially the myths and legends of the native people. Maybe he could get some room by a fire in exchange for a story or two. The season might be especially good for the tale his father used to tell him about Jack of the Lantern. He smiled as he suddenly noticed the few jack o' lanterns he saw here and there, candles flickering behind their carved faces.

Somewhere between two and four blocks later, the back of John's neck tingled. At four-and-a-half blocks, John knew for certain he was being followed. He quickened his pace and fingered the club he kept in a hidden pocket sewn into the inside of his coat. He didn't break into a run or even a jog, but he might as well have. He glanced back. Just as he thought, his pursuers had been surprised by John's increase in speed. They'd become careless in their haste to keep up.

This was where he decided if it was a matter of fight or flight.

He spotted the four of them without any trouble. Four was two too many. Two, he could fight long enough to discourage. Three was pushing it. Four wasn't even worth trying. He'd just wind up making them angry, and the beating would be even worse.

"Now, now, Johnny O'Brien," said a familiar voice. "We saw you give the beggar something. If you did that, then you've got something to spare for us, too."

Thomas was a big lad who led a gang of four other slightly-less-big lads. They'd been giving John trouble for years, even when they had been schoolboys together. And while Thomas was correct – John still did have the last gold coin of his family's treasure – Thomas and his fellows couldn't comprehend that John had no intention of ever spending it. Nor could they comprehend that a person might give their last coin over to a stranger with less fortune for no other reason than it was the decent thing to do.

Since John had only seen four of them, it meant that Paddy had either been left behind or that the other four were driving John toward the meanest, and least bright, of all of them. John turned on his toe and ran to the other side of the street. He might not be as big or strong as the members of Thomas's little mob of miscreants, but John was no weakling. Most of the work he could find as an Irishman involved heavy labor, the kind few others wanted. He also had practice outrunning gangs like this.

"Don't make it harder on yourself than you need to, Johnny Boy," Thomas called after him. "Just give it over, and we'll be off on our merry one way and you can go t'other."

John reached the other side of the street and scrambled up a fence between two buildings. He stopped at the top and looked back. Sure enough, Paddy was running from the direction John had just been heading.

"Sod off!" John called back.

Thomas and the others were not known for being clever or quick witted. They were even less so when angry. John had used taunts and teasing to great effect in escaping these five ruffians many times before. They hadn't ever seemed to catch on to it, and John would keep exploiting this weakness until they did.

Thomas called back something unflattering about John's mother as John dropped down the other side of the fence. John didn't much care. He'd never allowed people's words to affect him.

John found himself in an alley that had been converted to a storage area. Stacks of boxes lined both sides of the alley. John pursed his lips and he squinted with his right eye. In the space of a single breath, a plan formed. He had enough of a lead. Between the darkness in the alley and his pursuers' lack of imagination, the plan should work.

He ran to the other end of the alley, pushed some snow off the fence there, and then backtracked, making sure to walk backward through his own footprints. When he got back to where he'd climbed over, John squeezed in between two stacks of boxes. He clenched his teeth together to keep them from chattering.

The moment after John squeezed all the way back, he heard crunches in the snow where someone landed. Two more followed.

"He's gone to the other end," Thomas said.

A fourth person landed this side of the fence. Footsteps crunched toward the far end of the alley. A fifth person dropped down.

"Hurry up, you daft fool," one of them called from the other end of the alley.

The fifth person over the fence, likely Paddy, grunted something and started after his friends.

John remained huddled, shivering, keeping his teeth from shattering. He had to be sure they had actually fallen for his trick.

He counted to fifty before he crawled back out.

"There he is," one of them said from the far end. "Told you asking that man was smart."

John was up and over the fence even before he could waste time being scared or worrying about his plan failing. He landed and would have been off at a dead run, except someone was standing in his way.

John blinked several times to make sure he was actually seeing what he thought he was seeing. It wasn't a person at all.

The thing in front of him could only be a demon, like the ones from the stories his father had told him before he'd died. Despite its fine clothes, the thing was sorely out of place with its red skin and single horn that curled back behind its ear. It held a device that vented steam and arched lighting between two metal rods.

"It's a pleasure to make your acquaintance, John O'Brien," the thing said in a whiny and grating voice. "It took us quite a while to find you. We're still learning our way around this new continent."

The imp – it had to be an imp, in the stories imps were the little red ones – did some things to the device, and the lightning arched faster between the two rods. Behind him, on the other side of the fence, John heard the *psshh* of escaping air and what sounded like gears grinding.

"Ummm," John said, still trying to wrap his mind around the idea that the stories might be true.

The crack and snap of wood joined the other sounds. Then came a deluge of prayers: "Saints in heaven preserve us," "Mary, mother of god," and, "Though I walk through the valley of darkness."

"It seems your friends are getting acquainted with my Steam Soldiers." The imp winked at John. "Nothing personal, Jack my boy. You just happened to be born into the wrong family."

Thoughts raced through John's mind. The top two were that he hated being called Jack and that the imp's strange device couldn't be good. As the imp kept flicking switches and turning dials, the noises behind John got louder and more frequent. That could not be good.

"You got my name right the first time," John said, and pulled his club out of its secret pocket. The oak club was sixteen inches long and an inch and a half thick. John held it firmly with his thumb and first two fingers.

The imp flicked more switches and dials, and John heard several terrified and pained screams behind him along with a giant crash of shattering wood. He didn't look, but did suspect, that noise was the fence coming down.

John rushed forward and snapped the club at the device three times. One of the dials came off at the first snap. With the second, one of the e-lectrodes bent at an awkward angle and sparks buzzed away from the thing, fading into the night. The third strike never landed. By that time, the imp had caught on and spun out of the way.

In its haste to protect the device, the imp turned its back on John. John couldn't help but grin. He shifted his grip on the club, gripping it firmly with all five fingers. He pulled the club back behind his shoulder, and falling to one knee as he struck, John put all his body behind the blow to the imp's knee.

Now, John didn't know if the length of wood would actually hurt a demon, but he had to try. Just like with Thomas's ruffians, the demon and whatever was coming up behind him wasn't going to get John without as much effort as John could force them to make.

The club met the imp's knee with the expected resistance and the same crunch of bones and *pop* of cartilage that John was used to. John didn't like fighting. Fighting was the last resort, because in most situations he got a little banged up at the very least. Unless, that is, he caught his opponent completely off guard like this and got away before they could get up.

The imp writhed on the ground holding his leg and whimpering in pain. John spared a glance over his shoulder. Massive metallic men that looked like someone had turned a dozen locomotives into suits of armor stood over Thomas and his ruffians. The gang lay in much the same state as the imp, on the ground, groaning in pain. The armored things that stood over them had electrodes protruding from their joints, and those e-lectrodes buzzed and popped the same way the imp's device had after John had hit it.

John supposed those would be the Steam Soldiers.

Without a second thought, John took two steps and grabbed the device. The imp still had enough wherewithal to keep a tight grip.

"No," the imp said.

"Ah," John replied. "Yes."

John pulled harder, but the imp would not let go.

"Fine." John nearly snarled the word in his frustration.

John shifted the grip on his club to two fingers again. He snapped the club twice: first to the imp's nose and then to the wrist below the hand holding the controller. The imp's fingers opened. John snatched the box and considered for a moment what to do with it.

He almost took the thing with him. Then he thought better of it. It wasn't too heavy, but it would get heavier and heavier as he ran. Also, he might be able to hide, and then these things might go away. If he took the device that controlled the armored things, whoever owned these Steam Soldiers would definitely come after him and they wouldn't stop until they got it back.

"This seems to be pretty important," John said, waving the steaming and buzzing controller above the whimpering imp. "Have fun getting it."

With that, John lobbed it up onto the roof of a building on the other side of the street, turned, and started running. He got maybe ten steps before he heard cackling laughter above and behind him.

John skidded to a stop in the snow. There was another one on the roof. Probably lots of other ones. That would figure. It was that kind of night.

He looked back over his shoulder. Sure enough, he saw an odd-shaped shadow holding a thing that flashed and popped. Moments later, other odd-shaped shadows appeared on that rooftop and the other rooftops overlooking the street.

The Steam Soldiers started moving again, coming toward John. One pointed an arm at John. The wrist erupted in steam and fire, and the thing's hand flew at John. It missed him by less than a foot. Instead of his head, arm, or shoulder, the metal hand closed around a pole supporting the porch of a haberdasher shop. Wood groaned and splintered under the grip.

Then John noticed the chain strung between the metal arm and the metal hand.

He didn't wait to see the pole come flying away from the building.

He ran headlong into the night. He heard steam venting, electricity popping, and heavy footsteps stomping behind him. Oh, and crashing wood and shattering glass.

As he zigzagged down the street, two thoughts occupied John's mind. First, where could he hide? Second, what terrible thing had he done to warrant this? Thomas and his gang was one thing, but demons and armored soldiers controlled by some steam and electric box? This would be laughable were he not living it. So instead of laughing, he ran.

After two blocks, he grabbed a street lamp and used that to spin to the right without losing any of his speed. Normally, a series of quick turns would be the surest way to confuse, confound, and otherwise conceal himself from pursuit. However, that was all contingent upon his pursuers actually being human. John was halfway down the block and very certain he could get to the other end and out of sight, when two of those Steam Soldiers came crashing through a storefront not ten paces back.

With nothing readily available to help him alter his course, John slid a bit in the snow and then dashed toward the alley on the opposite side of the street. He really didn't want to go into some place that confined, but better that than possibly having one of those things burst out of a building right next to him.

And so the chase went on for longer than John could recall. He wove through alleys and side streets so much that he lost track of where he was. His lungs burned, his legs ached, and it felt like someone had stabbed him repeatedly in his left side. Behind him, demons cackled, Steam Soldiers hissed, buzzed, and clanked, and buildings broke under the weight of their pursuit. Running was no longer an option, but at least he wasn't cold anymore.

Soon John was reduced to a loping jog. Even though he was used to long hours of strenuous work, he couldn't keep up that level of headlong flight indefinitely. Head down, body aching, his mind raced for some way to escape.

He came around a corner and found himself staring at the bakery. The beggar still sat huddled in the doorway, soaking up what heat he could.

"This is wrong," John said to himself in short gasps.

John was sure he'd been moving steadily away from here. Yet, here he was. It didn't make sense. But then, so little about this night did. He was about to turn and flee again when two of the metal monstrosities crashed through the bakery. The building groaned and collapsed, part of it on the beggar. John could hear the beggar's cries of pain, although muffled from the boards.

Then a loud *whoomph* came from inside the rubble that was once a bakery, and a giant flame erupted from the center of the wood. The blaze spread quickly.

That gave John an idea.

Most people wouldn't do anything to help someone getting beaten or murdered in the street. They would turn a blind eye and deaf ear to all the crashing and breaking wood. Oh, they might look out their window, but they'd never actually do anything to stop it, even if they didn't believe that it was real and not some strange dream. However, there was one thing almost no one would ignore.

"Fire!" John yelled with all the strength he could muster.

His voice wasn't very loud because he was panting and puffing from running, but it was loud enough that the demons stopped cackling and the

Steam Soldiers stopped moving. That gave John just enough incentive to fill his lungs and yell again.

"Fire!"

This time, people opened windows and stuck their heads out into the cold night air. Other people took up the cry.

It wasn't until after people started shouting and rushing into the street that John considered that if these things wanted him so much, they might be willing to hurt any bystanders like they had Thomas's gang. As more and more people took up the cry of "fire," the demons and their metal soldiers fled into the night.

John only allowed himself a small sigh of relief before he was moving again, this time across the street. When he reached the remains of the bakery, the beggar had gone from crying out in pain to moaning. The fire had reached him and caught on the beggar's ragged coat.

People rushed about, and in the distance John heard the *clang, clang, clang* of the fire brigade bell. Fire was the one threat nobody would ignore.

John began clearing debris off the beggar, and within moments other people were helping him. When they'd gotten the beggar free, his right arm was engulfed in flames up to his shoulder. Before anyone could offer suggestions or advice, John rolled the beggar off the porch and into a snow bank. The flames sputtered out with a sharp *hiss.*

"I'm going to get him to a doctor," John said. He knew where one was only a few blocks away.

Before anyone else could protest, John lifted the beggar up and hurried away. He had, in a moment, weighed the risk of staying with the crowd and having them ask questions against moving on and encountering the demons again. At this point there were dozens – perhaps more than a hundred – people up and about to help deal with the fire. As the cry went out, more and more would be up. It was a fairly good gamble that John was safe for at least the rest of this night. Besides, the beggar had been hurt because of him. Others probably had too, but John could help this man right now.

Soon, John was pounding on the door of the doctor's office. A minute or so later, he heard locks rattle and the door open about two inches. A single eye glared at John from behind a spectacle.

"Sir," John said, "this man is hurt."

The eye looked at the beggar and back at John. The door opened. John entered and placed the beggar on the long table that filled the center of the room.

The doctor was short and frail, with only a few wisps of hair on the top of his head. While the doctor wore a night shirt, John noticed that he also had on trousers and shoes. Perhaps he'd heard the call for fire and was getting ready to go out and see if anyone required his services.

"Can you pay?" the doctor asked.

"Pay?" John replied. "This man may be dying and you're asking about money?"

"This is a business, son," the doctor said, "not a charity. If you have no means to compensate me for my work, I suggest you take him to Saint Mary's Church. The sisters there care for the sick and injured among the homeless."

"St. Mary's is halfway to the other side of Boston," John said, his voice rising. "He probably wouldn't survive me carrying him all that way."

The doctor shrugged. John looked from the beggar to the doctor, and back to the beggar. Tonight was quickly being burned into John's mind as the very worst night of his life since his parents died Halloween night almost three years ago. He couldn't even make it into a great story to trade for food or shelter because nobody would believe it.

"Fine," John said. "This should cover it."

He slipped the last gold coin of his family's treasure out of his glove and held it out to the doctor. The doctor eyed the coin, nodded, and held out his hand. John placed the coin gently on the doctor's palm, and after a moment, let go.

The instant John's fingers left the coin, a light brighter than any lamp, lantern, or candle filled the room. The beggar rolled off the table and stood straight and tall, no longer hunched over as he had been. The grime and muck that clung to his face seemed to be burned away by the light. The coat that was more rags than garment fluttered in a wind John did not feel and transformed into a pristine white robe. Two pearl-white wings sprouted from the beggar's shoulder blades.

While the beggar underwent this transformation, the doctor had pulled off the night shirt to reveal a priest's collar.

"John O'Brien," the doctor-turned-priest said, "meet Saint Peter."

John blinked. "Even with the night I've had, that was unexpected."

Three

John O'Brien stood looking back and forth at the priest and the man introduced as Saint Peter. Make that: the man with wings and who was e-mitting a continuous white light who had been introduced as Saint Peter. John closed his eyes, but even then the light shone through his eyelids, like looking into the sun with one's eyes closed.

"That's just grand," said a decidedly feminine voice from slightly behind John. Her Irish accent was as thick and heavy as anyone who had just stepped off the boat from the old country. "Very nicely done gents, easing him into things like that."

John spun around, bringing his club into his hand.

"Put it away, O'Brien," said a young woman. "What is it with the men in this family and their sticks?"

The young lady carried a plain wooden chair that looked as if it were made right from the branches of a tree without much in the way of sanding or polishing. It also looked as old, frail, and weathered as Saint Peter had when he'd been a beggar. Behind her, the door to the back of the doctor's office swung closed.

The girl herself looked to be of an age with John, from seventeen to nineteen years old – John himself was eighteen. She had blondish hair with more than a hint of brown within it, and her eyes were the brightest green. She wore a coat that was only slightly more together than the rags Saint Peter had worn as a beggar. The style of the coat was completely unknown to John. Long and pleated, with flaring at the waist and what had once been a long row of buttons, of which only three remained.

Remembering his manners, John tipped his hat to her. "Miss."

"Mr. Obrien," she said with a comforting smile. "I'm your cousin, Moira. Moira O'Neil. This is going to be a lot to take in. Please, have a seat."

She placed the chair down just behind him.

At the mention of sitting, the exhaustion of his flight from the demons came crashing back. John sat with a relieved sigh.

"Thank you," John said. "I don't recall my parents ever mentioning any relations among the O'Neils."

"That's because they didn't know about us," Moira said. "We're rather far removed, but we could each trace our line back through the centuries to the same penultimate grandfather."

"Alright," John said. "A pleasure to meet you, cousin Moira O'Neil, and Your...um...Holiness?"

"Peter is fine." The saint's voice was soft, yet seemed to fill the room.

"And this," Moira said, indicating the priest, "is Father McDermott."

The priest came forward and shook John's hand.

"It is a great pleasure, young man," the Father said.

"Glad to meet you all," John said, then before any of them could say anything else, John regarded Saint Peter. "Are you aware that there are a bunch of demons running around Boston? Oh, and they have a bunch of big metal men they call Steam Soldiers that shoot their hands at things and crash through buildings. Oh, and do you have any idea why they are after me, personally, by name?"

"It is exactly because of this that we have sought you out," Saint Peter said. "We've been seeking you for quite some time. The forces of darkness actually did us a favor by leading us to you."

"Oh, well," John said, "the next time I see them, I'll be sure to thank them. And why are you all looking for me in the first place?"

"You are one of the last three descendants of Jack of the Lantern," Father McDermott said.

On any other night, John probably would have laughed, laughed hard. Tonight he took them all in, one at a time. Saint Peter stood looking, well, serene and saintly. Father McDermott gave the impression of the kindly uncle or grandfather. Moira gave him a slight smile that seemed to say, "I know exactly how you feel." John opened his mouth to say something, decided that he didn't really have anything to say that might be appropriate in front of a priest, let alone a saint, so he closed his mouth again, sighed, and shrugged.

After a moment of silence, John decided he did have something to say. "Of course I am. And my mother was the Tooth Fairy. We would have the Easter Bunny and Santa Claus over for tea every third Sunday of the month, oh, and we'd sit at the Round Table, as the family was charged with keeping it safe for Arthur's eventual return. We even kept Excalibur in my father's study for the occasion."

Father McDermott took a step forward and wagged his finger at John. "Look here, young man, I know this has been a trying night for you, but that is no way to speak to—"

"Oh, shut it Father," Moira said, stepping between the priest and John. "If the young man is going to lip off to a saint of heaven, he's not bloody likely to fall into line by having you wiggle your finger at him. Wouldn't you agree, Peter?"

27

"Quite right," Saint Peter replied.

The Saint did not look in the least bit perturbed at John's outburst. Which, after John considered it for a moment, made a certain sort sense.

"It's the truth John," Moira said. "I know it must sound crazy, even with everything that's happened. I had the benefit of growing up knowing, but I can prove it's all real."

"That should be interesting," John said. "Go ahead."

"I'm sure your parents told you stories," Moira said. "There were many stories of Jack of the Lantern. But I'll wager that your parents told you which three things Jack wished for from Saint Peter. Go ahead and name them, in order, in the manner of the story."

John looked from Moira to Saint Peter. Saint Peter smiled and nodded. "If you know the story, this should be easy enough."

John knew the story. This was the season when he traded the story for food and possibly shelter.

"This here, my chair," John recited, and Moira spoke the words exactly with him, with the exact same inflections, "anyone that sit in it cannot get up from it until I give them leave to do so."

He paused and looked back and forth between his cousin, the Father, and the saint. Peter extended his right hand in an invitation to continue. John did so, his cousin keeping pace with him again.

"This here, my coat, anyone that take hold of it cannot let go of it until I give them leave to do so. And this here, my smithing hammer, anyone that take hold of it cannot stop smithing with it until I give them but leave to do so." When he finished, John paused, looked at Moira, and said, "So, we know the same story. What does that prove?"

John did not like Moira's self-satisfied smirk, not one bit.

"Try to get up," Moira said.

And that's the moment John O'Brien believed, just as he believed that he wasn't going to be able to get up. He sat in the ancient looking chair glaring at his cousin.

"Should I even bother without being given leave?" he asked.

"Big, strong young man such as yourself shouldn't need anyone's permission to get his feet underneath him and stand up."

John clicked his tongue and sighed. "Going to force this are we?"

Moira shrugged.

John tried to stand. As hard as he pushed against the floor, he could not rise. He didn't struggle against the force holding him in the chair very long. For one, he was too tired. For two, he didn't see the point in a struggle that would avail him nothing. For three, he didn't want to give his new-found cousin any further reason to gloat at him. Then John realized something, and his heart began to speed up.

"If the story of Jack of the Lantern is true, then I'll bet the story of the ritual to keep the Devil's Gate closed is true, too. But it's not Halloween yet, and there are demons running around. Something happened, something bad, both to Jack and the ladies that keep the gate closed."

At that, the smirk slid from Moira's face as her lips pressed together. Her eyes welled with tears.

"Only to one of them," Moira said. "The younger one made it out."

"I'm sorry," Jack said, and he was. He missed his mother and father terribly. If Moira was the granddaughter in this generation of the two women who kept the Devil's Gate closed, then the only people she really knew were her grandmother and Jack of the Lantern. "But something must have happened to Jack, or he would have chased the demons back into Hell with his lantern. Isn't that what he does with the stragglers on Halloween?" John knew he was repeating himself, but that was normal – repetition was part of his process of sorting through things. Moira looked like she was going to say something, but John held up his hand and wagged it at her. "What happened to him? Something happened, and that's bad, but it's important to something right now." Realization dawned on John. "He's not here to let me out of the chair."

And despite his logical understanding of the situation and that he couldn't get out of the chair without Jack of the Lantern to give leave to do so, John squirmed and struggled to get out. He thrashed back and forth for a few moments.

"You've leave to get out of my chair," Moira said.

As soon as she spoke those words, the force holding John to the seat of the chair vanished. His struggles carried him off the chair and onto the floor in a huff. Moira offered her hand. Using her as a counterbalance, with a groan, John stood.

He wanted to be angry at Moira, but he understood why she did it. He'd have never really believed her otherwise and would have left if he'd had the means.

"Alright," John said. "So we've determined that all the stories my parents told me are actually our secret family history. What's that got to do with the here and now, demons coming after me, and you three showing up looking for me? What's so special about me?"

"Just by being of the line of Jack of the Lantern gives the demons cause to fear you," Saint Peter said. "As a descendant of Jack's blood, he can grant you the ability to use the objects he wished of me all those centuries ago, as he has given the coat and chair to Moira. They will also fear that you may have inherited Jack's cleverness and cunning. By all observations, you may have all that he ever had, and more."

29

"And you want me to help," John said. "Really, there has to be someone better, smarter, stronger, or braver, perhaps all of them. I'm really mostly a coward."

"You think too little of yourself," Saint Peter said, "but also too much."

"Your family history lends weight to what must be done," Father McDermott said. "It will be so much harder for someone not of Jack's line to do what must be done."

"And what's that?" John asked.

"Nothing too difficult," Moira said. "Just scare the Devil and all his kin back into Hell long enough for me to complete the ritual that will repair and close the Devil's Gate."

"Oh, is that all?" John said. "I think I can do that."

Four

Moira eyed her cousin. He looked so much like Jack of the Lantern: plain face, green eyes, and hair that could be blond, auburn, or brown depending on the light. Even bundled in his coat and scarf against the cold, she could tell he was used to physical work. His right eye also squinted the same way Jack of the Lantern's did when he was trying to remember something or was about to play some clever trick on Grandmother.

Moira turned her head away and wiped a tear. Even after nearly three years since the Devil's Gate came down, she still missed her grandmother, and after the sacrifice Grandmother's life had been, she deserved a better end than she'd received at the hands of the demons.

"You alright?" John asked.

"Right as rain," Moira replied. When she faced John again, he wasn't squinting. He was looking at her, his head tilted to the side, his mouth formed into a worried frown. "Really, I'm fine."

"You're suddenly being very reasonable about this, John," Father McDermott said. "I have to admit, I expected a bit of protest."

John looked from Moira to the priest.

"I considered it," John said. "But what would be the point? It's not like I'm going to tell Saint Peter, *no*."

"Well, you could," Saint Peter said. "I'm not here to force you into anything, John. It's just that you and your cousins are the natural choices for this task. There's power in the fear that dark creatures around the world have for your penultimate grandfather."

"They didn't seem to fear me," John said. "Quite the opposite."

"If they didn't fear you," Saint Peter replied, "they would have left you well enough alone. They would have left your entire family well e-

31

nough alone, instead of killing all but three of you on All Hallow's Eve three years ago."

"Wait right there. Halloween? Three years ago?"

"Yes," Saint Peter said.

"That's the night my parents died. Everyone thought they were murdered by a thief."

"No, John," Moira said. "They were killed by the demons, just like my grandmother."

Both of John's eyes grew very narrow, and he looked off to his left, seemingly at nothing at all.

"Oh yes, I think I can do that." John's tone held none of the flip-ancy it had the first time he'd said it. "Where do we start?"

"Well," Saint Peter said. "Before anything else, we must attend to the business of your wishes."

"Wishes?" John asked.

"Don't you pay attention to the old stories at all on this side of the Atlantic?" Father McDermott asked. "Of course you get wishes. You gave the last coin of your family's treasure to save a man you did not know from Adam for no other reason than it was the good and decent thing to do."

"Other people do nice things all the time," John said. "They don't get wishes."

"But they don't commit selfless acts of sacrifice for saints in disguise," Moira said. "It's kind of one of the Old Laws. I don't understand it, and I'm not sure the saints and angels and all of them understand it, but that's the way it is. Just like the Dark One and his demons cannot break a bargain fairly made."

"Really?" John said, and his right eye squinted again. "Three wishes you say?"

"Yes," Saint Peter replied. "Three, and only three. I've been on this continent enough to know how you Americans try to think around corners and be terribly clever. I'll not grant you any more wishes."

"Oh, that's fine," John said. "I've already got my wishes in mind, but let me think about them for a bit."

"Take your time," Saint Peter said. "They are three very important decisions."

With that, John began to wander about the room, seemingly at random. He muttered under his breath as he wove this way and that. Moira tried to make out some of the words, but couldn't. She watched him. The more he walked, the faster his muttering became, and his right eye eventually closed completely which seemed to scrunch John's face up with the strain of keeping it closed as tight as possible.

All of a sudden, in mid-mumble and mid-step, John stopped. His right eye opened, and he looked at Saint Peter.

"Any specific things I'm going to have to do in this process? Or am I on my own?"

"You will not be alone," Saint Peter replied. "There will be three of you. Moira, and your cousin Daniel."

"Why three of us?" John asked. "The demons are sure to try and stop us. Why should all of us take the risk?"

"Because power exists in numbers," Father McDermott explained. "Three is a very powerful number when placed in opposition against the forces of Darkness."

John nodded. "Oh, yes. I can see the sense in that." He turned away from them. "Alright, I have to start thinking in the way of the old stories." He paced a little more then stopped again. "Anything else I should know?"

"That's all that I can think of," Saint Peter said. "Either of you?"

"I don't think so," Father McDermott said. "We've pretty much covered it."

"There is something else," Moira said.

John looked at her, and sighed. "What is it?"

Moira felt for John and how overwhelmed he must have been at that moment. She felt the same. Well, perhaps not quite as much, as she knew more about what was going on. Then again, she knew how difficult the other thing they needed to do was going to be.

"Once we scare the Devil and his kin back into Hell, we've got to be able to keep the Devil's Gate closed. I know the ritual, but I only have one of the artifacts. We'll need to get replacements for the others."

"And let me guess, each one is an extremely rare object and is going to be almost as difficult to get as chasing the Devil back into Hell."

Moira nodded.

"Of course it is."

John took a deep breath, let it out, and with shoulders slumped forward he continued pacing. Again, as he traversed the room, seemingly at random, John's right eye squinted and his mouth scrunched up.

He seemed to pace around the room for at least an hour, though Moira had no means by which to tell how much time had actually passed. Her legs grew tired, and she hopped up onto the doctor's table in the center of the room. She could have sat in the chair that Jack had given her, all she had to do was give herself leave to stand up, but she couldn't bring herself to do it. That chair had been the center of far too much trickery and deceit over the centuries.

Father McDermott came to lean on the table next to her. He opened his mouth to speak, but even before he could form that first sound into a syllable, John sent a silencing *hsst* from across the room. He did have the decency to blush just a little when the priest glared at him, and John even murmured an apologetic, "Sorry Father, but I'm thinking hard. Doesn't come naturally to me," and then went back to pacing.

Finally, John stopped. He looked at Saint Peter. "I'm ready to make my wishes. But I need to make them in private."

"Why private?" Moira asked.

"Because at least one of them is a surprise," John said. "And I hate to ruin surprises."

"The wishes are John's, and he is entitled to make them alone," Saint Peter said. "If you will join me in the next room."

"Absolutely!" John went to the door and held it open for Saint Peter.

"We'll be back in a few moments," Saint Peter said, and went into the other room.

John nodded at Father McDermott. Then he looked at Moira. John's mouth curled into a self-satisfied smirk, and he gave her a conspiratorial wink.

"We'll be out when we're done," John said, "but it might take more than a few minutes."

With that, John followed Saint Peter, shutting the door behind them.

Moira and Father McDermott looked at each other.

"He's a cheeky one," Father McDermott said.

"Yes he is," Moira said with a hint of smile.

John O'Brien was definitely amusing, in a defiant sort of way, but she hadn't decided whether she liked him or not. She wanted to think it might be because he was American, but she hadn't known much of anyone outside of the cottage she'd grown up in. Even in the last three years, she'd only been with Father McDermott, and of course Saint Peter after she'd given her last coin to a beggar, a beggar that just happened to be a saint in disguise. They'd been so busy searching for John that Moira hadn't had many opportunities to get to know how people acted on a day-to-day basis. However, she did know that John seemed a bit more flippant than she suspected most people were.

"What now?" Moira asked.

"We wait until John makes his wishes," Father McDermott said, and leaned back against the wall.

Moira sat on the table, swinging her legs back and forth. She didn't have a watch, so to count the passing time, she began to count the number of swings her legs made. She expected Saint Peter and John to come out somewhere between one hundred and one hundred fifty.

At two hundred seventy-seven she heard Saint Peter's raised voice cry out, "That's not how it's done!"

Her legs froze underneath the table. She glanced at Father McDermott. The Father stood ramrod straight and glared at the door. From the beet-red color that washed over his face, she didn't need to guess what the priest thought of John, at least not right then. After a few moments they heard no other outbursts, and so Moira went back to swinging her legs.

At three hundred twenty-six, the door from the back room opened. Light from Saint Peter's glow spilled into the room. Had it been natural light, Moira probably would have been blinking, momentarily blinded. John came out, heading straight for the front door. His smirk was gone, but his eyes sparkled with mischievous delight.

"Are we ready, then?" Father McDermott asked.

"Oh, not by half," John replied as he walked across the room to the front door. "Sit tight. I've a quick errand to run. Return in a moment." He headed out into the snow and cold.

Moira craned her neck to look back in the room where John and Saint Peter had been speaking. Saint Peter stood in the doorway looking where John had just left. The saint's wings had wrapped around his shoulders, as if comforting him. Other than that, Saint Peter just blinked after John.

"It doesn't sound like it's going at all well," Father McDermott said.

"I wouldn't say that," Saint Peter replied. "He's much more than we expected, so much more. I believe he will either live up to Jack of the Lantern's legacy, or he will doom the world to live in darkness for a century or two."

"That's not very encouraging," Father McDermott said.

"It's not?" Saint Peter asked.

"How could that be encouraging in any way?"

"Moment to moment, the young man is as clever and cunning as Jack was on the best days of his life," Saint Peter explained. "He is bold, daring, refuses to be cowed by the fact he is hunted by demons, and has bargained the details of three wishes with a saint, all in the same night. Nothing great in this world has ever been achieved without some risk. He has a scheme. He's shared some of the details with me, though I don't think I know even half of it. Even with the parts I do know, I told him that the chances of it succeeding were infinitesimal. Would you like to know what he said in response?"

Moira and Father McDermott both nodded.

"He said, 'My country wouldn't exist if men paid attention to that way of thinking,' and went back to browbeating me about exactly what he should and should not be granted from each individual wish. Normally, the moment anyone begins attempting to haggle the finer points of saintly providence, it would invalidate the whole business, but everything John is arguing for, as mad as his plan is, is so that it has a chance of success. As brash and irreverent as he is, he's a fine young man. It will indeed be interesting to see if things play out in his favor."

"Is it wise to gamble the whole of humanity on his sliver of a chance?" Father McDermott asked.

"Well," Moira said. "It's not like we haven't been here before, humanity that is. How many disasters have we heard about in the old stories where we barely survive one disaster or another because of one human's courage, or wit, or strength?" She looked at Saint Peter. "Sometimes it's the trying that's the most important part, isn't it?"

Saint Peter smiled at her. "Your words have the ring of some truth, but not all of it. Yes, some of it is in the attempting, but a large part of it is in who makes the attempt and why. And of course, the chance of failure always exists, because were there not the chance for failure, then it really wouldn't be worthy of becoming a story."

"Is this one of those moments that will become a story centuries from now?" Moira asked. "Will people speak of John O'Brien and Moira O'Neil as they do of Jack of the Lantern?"

"I have many a blessing given to me as a saint, dear child," Saint Peter replied, "but prophesy is not one of them. That ability belongs to a different saint entirely."

"Well, can you go and ask that saint if my plan is going to work?" John said from the door. He held a jack o' lantern in his left hand. This lantern was carved from a pumpkin. Its eyes and nose were triangles, and it had a wide, jagged-toothed grin.

"Where did you get that?" Father McDermott demanded.

John shrugged. "I found it lying around."

"You stole it," McDermott said.

John shrugged again. "Look. You want me to do this thing, this *very* big thing that apparently no one else can do. Well then, you've got to let me do it my way. And, in my way, I needed a jack o' lantern, and we don't have time for me to get one – not that I can afford one anyway – and carve it myself. Besides, the face on this one is better than I could do myself." John looked at Saint Peter. "Shall we conclude our business?"

"Indeed, we shall," Saint Peter replied.

They went into the other room, leaving Father McDermott behind, mouth agape. Moira covered her mouth as if yawning, when in truth she was hiding her smile. Like Moira, the Father hadn't gotten out into the world very much. He maintained the parish and provided services in the wilds of Ireland, close enough to the place between places so that the ladies of Jack's line who maintained watch over the Devil's Gate could attend. A few other families, who had all lived in the area for countless generations, attended services there as well, but all of them maintained the strict public civility that Moira had noticed lacking in many people they'd met in larger communities.

After a few moments, Father McDermott composed himself. "I believe I need a breath of air and a bit of pipe. Call for me when they come back out."

"Yes, Father," Moira said, and went back to swinging her legs.

It took considerably less time, only ninety-four leg swings, before the door opened again.

This time, the room beyond was dark. The only light was moonlight from the room's single window and the faint glow of candlelight flickering a few feet back from the doorway. The candles flickered behind the face of the jack o' lantern that John had *found*. John held the lantern in his left hand and his stick in his right. He stepped into the room. His stick was now etched with silver and iron crosses. His coat had changed, becoming nearly a twin of her coat, except where hers was plain brown wool, John's coat was black wool striped with orange...was that silk? While he hadn't changed in size, he seemed bigger than he had before. No...bigger was the wrong word. He looked like Jack of the Lantern had. A legend made flesh. His smirk had changed. While still containing a bit of its original mischievousness, now it also held more than a hint of malicious humor.

They stayed there a few moments, looking at each other, Moira taking in the sight of her changed cousin, and she supposed John was getting used to what had changed within him.

Father McDermott came back in and stopped short. He blinked a few times at the sight of John, then looked around.

"Where's Saint Peter?" Father McDermott asked.

"Gone. He's done what he can. Now the rest is up to us."

"Well then, John," Father McDermott said, "what's with this outfit?"

"I'm not John anymore. The name's Jack."

"Of course," Moira said. "You took up the mantle of Jack of the Lantern."

"Oh no. Jack of the Lantern is still trapped in the Dark One's keeping. I couldn't do what needs doing if I called myself Jack of the Lantern. The demons aren't terrified of him anymore. They might be nervous, but they've learned they can beat him. No. I'm someone new, someone they will learn to fear far more than nice, gentle, and reasonable Jack of the Lantern.

He paused, and his smile grew from a smirk to wide, frightening grin.

"My name is Halloween Jack. Let's go scare some demons."

Five

The last three years hadn't been the kindest Jack of the Lantern had ever lived through. Still, with all the pain and suffering the demons had inflicted upon him, when they stopped even for a second, Jack of the Lantern would look at them and say, "Not bad. But how many centuries did you cower in fear of me. Let me out of this cage and we'll see how things go." In the first year, every time he said that, they'd torture him more. He'd say it again when they stopped. And so it went in a vicious circle.

Things began to slow down in the second year, after the Devil and his kin took over Buckingham Palace. They stuck his cage in a corner of the throne room, occasionally poking at him with something sharp or hot or both. From his cage, Jack of the Lantern watched, helpless, as the embodiment of everything that was evil in western culture sat on the British throne and conquered the empire with their Steam Soldiers.

Then in the third year, a few weeks before All Hallow's Eve, things began to get entertaining again. Oh, they still tormented him, and as things got worse for them, so did their torments. But what was a bit of pain and discomfort compared to watching the Dark Lord's eyes twitch with that same level of frustration from the centuries before the gate fell? It all started when a familiar looking imp crept into the throne room, shoulders slumped as if it were trying to fold in on itself. Jack of the Lantern noticed, with no small amount of satisfaction, that it walked with a pronounced limp.

"What happened?" the Devil asked.

The imp cowered as he said, "We found the boy."

"Then where is the body?" the Devil ask. "You were supposed to kill him and lay his body at my feet."

"H-he got away," the imp said. "There was a fire, and people started coming out of their houses, and so we left him alone for the night. After learning a bit about the Americans, we felt it best not to reveal our presence on the very first night. We had him, and you taught us the virtue of patience."

"So what went wrong?"

"Well, Saint Peter came…"

"GET OUT!" the Devil bellowed with such fury that the force of his voice flung the imp out of the throne room.

Jack of the Lantern couldn't see it, but he heard something strike the wall beyond the doors, followed by a pained grunt.

The Devil turned to one of the hulking scorpion demons that flanked him as his guards.

"Take that wretched failure and cast him back to the other side of the Devil's Gate. He doesn't deserve to be on this side."

"Nooooo!" came a mournful cry out in the hall. "Master, I'll do anything!"

"You'll rot," the Devil said. "That's twice you've upset me concerning this family. And that's enough out of you, blacksmith."

It wasn't until the Devil mentioned it that Jack of the Lantern realized he was snickering. Jack stopped and gave a mocking bow to the Devil. Then Jack of the Lantern coughed. It was a long, hard cough, as if he was trying to eject something from deep in his chest. He had to grip the bars of his cage to steady himself. He took a breath…and coughed again – this time even longer and harder than before. He fell to his knees, and the third cough came. He'd expected it after the second. Ever since that first visit from Saint Peter, his life had been nothing but a continuous pattern of threes.

"What's wrong with you, Jack?" the Devil asked. "You can't get sick, and none of my kin have touched you."

"I don't think you should call me Jack anymore," the man said as he stood. Even as he said those words, he knew they were true. "I'm just John the Blacksmith. I think you have a brand new Jack to worry about."

As if speaking prophecy, a pack of little goblins with gray-green skin and orange-ish eyes scurried into the throne room. They prostrated themselves before the Dark One, and when he bid them rise, they fell to bickering on which of them would do the speaking. As was common in these situations, the smallest of all of them was pushed to the front of the group.

"Your Mighty Evilness," the goblin squeaked. It swallowed once and winced as it spoke, expecting the worst. "We may have a problem."

The Devil looked at John the Blacksmith who stood smiling in the cage. John could see himself reflected in the Devil's soulless eyes. He was now a short, stocky man, balding on top, but what was one to expect after all these centuries? More importantly, he had lost all sense of the legend that had once made him Jack of the Lantern.

The Devil's face pulled back into one terrible grimace as he rounded on the goblins.

"What. Happened."

John the Blacksmith already knew the answer. His family had happened.

The terrified little goblin opened his mouth to speak, but the Devil cut him off.

"Aren't there supposed to be thirteen goblins in a pack? I only count eleven."

"Um, yes, sir," the goblin said, his voice cracking. "They went home."

"Home?" The Devil blinked. "Home, where?"

"Back to Hell where it's safe," the goblin replied. "They said they'd rather go back than stay in a world with *him* in it."

"Him? Him who?"

"Halloween Jack, Your Fearfulness. He's worse than The Lantern ever was. Some of the others are more afraid of him than they are of you."

The foundations of Buckingham Palace shook with the Devil's fury, and John the Blacksmith, who had once been Jack of the Lantern, couldn't help but laugh.

*   *   *

Mixxplik, the goblin, had been so hungry for so long. He was the runt of his pack, and pickings were slim, both in Hell and in every year when they got to roam free on Halloween. So many people back then hid behind those blasted lanterns, and he was so small. Even after the Dark Lord had brought down the Devil's Gate and captured The Lantern, he'd ordered all his kin not to make too much of a nuisance of themselves, at least, not until they secured rulership over the whole world. Mixxplik could see the sense in that. Even with The Lantern trapped, mankind had many other ways of protecting themselves from the forces of darkness.

But tonight, Mixxplik wouldn't be hungry anymore. The pack leader had decided they were going to eat well. They'd found an orphanage at the edge of a good-sized town. The plan was for the pack to eat the children, clean their teeth with the bones, and burn the orphanage down to hide the fact. In the morning, the pack would hide in the trees and giggle while the rest of the town came and wept over the tragedy. All in all, it would be the best night the pack had had in centuries, and the best part: Mixxplik wouldn't go to sleep hungry in the morning.

As he crept down the chimney – he'd been chosen because he was the smallest – Mixxplik's mouth watered at the thought of sinking his sharp teeth into the nice, juicy thigh of an eight or nine-year-old. Yummy. If he was lucky, he'd get a boy. The puppy dog tails gave boys just the right hint of spicy. Girls were too sweet for his taste, what with all that sugar and niceness. But, that was in his imagination. In truth, he'd be happy with anything he got, even if it was some old and stringy teenager.

He came out of the chimney into a room full of sleeping children. Three rows of beds stretched the length of the room, one against each wall and one down the middle. The little snores and the whimpers of those trapped in nightmares tempted him. For most goblins, the cries of pain that came from food were just as much a part of eating as sinking fangs into flesh. However, Mixxplik resisted. If he started munching on one of the little morsels before the pack got them all collected, it would scare the others off, and then there wouldn't be enough food to go a-round. Always practical in his thinking, Mixxplik was.

Then Mixxplik heard a sound very out of place in a room filled with sleeping children. Someone, an older-than-a-child-sounding someone, cleared his throat. Yes, that deep throat-clearing definitely came from a he rather than a she. Then came the distinctive sound of a striking match, followed by the appearance of a flickering flame. Mixxplik knew he should run, but goblins had a weakness for bright things, almost as much as they had a weakness for soft, squirmy food. He watched the little flame weave and bob in the air, then it went out of sight. Whoever held the match had put it into something. Mixxplik could see the soft glow at the top of whatever it was. Then, whoever was holding the thing turned it a-round, and the thing turned out to be a jack o' lantern.

Mixxplik couldn't help but giggle. He kept it controlled and quiet, but he giggled nonetheless.

"Really?" he asked. "You think that's going to...?"

As Mixxplik looked into the eyes of the jack o' lantern, staring defiance at that symbol that all the denizens of Hell had feared for so many centuries, the light from its three candles filled his vision until he could see nothing but the flickering lights. He tore his gaze from the lant-ern, but those three flames continued to fill his vision so that he couldn't see anything else.

"Trap that one!" someone said, someone with an Irish accent. For some reason, Mixxplik felt it did not bode well.

A moment later something wrapped around him, enveloping him so much that he could not move his arms or legs.

"Strike, stick, strike," that same Irish-accented voice said, "with two fingers."

This is going to be very bad for me, Mixxplik thought.

And it was. Something thin and hard began to hit him. It hit him hard and fast, beating him about the joints. Demons and other creatures from the dark realms couldn't die, at least not in the human sense of dying. However being the runt of the pack, many times Mixxplik found himself wishing otherwise. He was fairly certain this would be one of those times.

As the beating continued, Mixxplik heard children waking up and crying out.

"Don't worry, children," a woman, also with an Irish accent, said. "That little beasty won't be able to hurt you. Yes, it's a goblin, but we've got it under control. You see that man in the corner? Don't look at the lantern. That would be bad." As Mixxplik had learned. Several of the children spoke, confirming that they did see the man in the corner. "Well, that man is named Halloween Jack, and he's the thing that ghosts and ghoolies and goblins and all the other dark beasties are scared of most. Now, see this goblin? There are a bunch more outside. Calm down. Halloween Jack is going to teach you how to get the goblins to leave and not come back."

"Stick, come back," the man said, and the beating stopped. "Alright children, we've only got time for me to tell you this once, or the goblins outside will get suspicious. There's a stick next to every bed. Grab yours. Good. Now, you all down there, yes, the biggest and oldest. Grab your blankets and put one under the window over there. When the goblin hops down onto it, wrap it up, take it to the middle of the room, and work it over with your sticks. Be careful to only hold the stick with your thumb and first two fingers, otherwise you'll hurt them too much."

"But they're goblins," a boy said. "Goblins eat children. Why do we have to be careful about how much we hurt them?"

"Excellent question," the man said, this Halloween Jack fellow. "If you hurt it too badly, it won't be able to run away. Then you're going to have figure out what to do with it. So, no time to waste. You lads, get ready. Open the window."

And from there, Mixxpik heard the rest of his pack getting captured and beaten. His beating resumed. He fought and struggled but couldn't wriggle free of whatever was confining him. After a few minutes of thumpings and goblins crying in pain, the children began to giggle. Mixxplik decided there was no worse sound than your food laughing at you while beating you with a stick.

After a time, a long, painful time later, the beating stopped.

"Coat return to me," the voice of Halloween Jack said.

The thing trapping Mixxplik slid off of him. He could see again. Mixxplik found himself amidst the rest of his pack. All the goblins lay around him, rolling and writhing in pain. They were next to the door leading outside; the door was open. Mixxplik looked toward the center of the room. The man stood there, wearing an ancient-looking coat of orange and black and holding the jack o' lantern and a wicked stick covered in crosses. The face of the jack o' lantern was now turned away from Mixxplik. Behind the man stood what looked like every child of the orphanage. Each child had a stick, and while the sticks weren't fancy with the crosses and such, those sticks made Mixxplik suddenly realize the wisdom of running away to fight, and eat, another day.

Halloween Jack said something else, but Mixxplik didn't listen; he was too busy running for the door.

It wasn't long before the rest of his pack caught up to him. As they fled, Mixxplik heard one of his packmates mutter, "I think I'm going to go back to Hell where it's safe."

* * *

Naberius, Marquis of Hell, couldn't help but smile at the long line of former Confederate soldiers that stretched out from his table. He'd set up this little meeting at a crossroads next to a reputedly very fine tavern. He'd spoken to the tavern keeper, a kindly man with a head of gray hair, about having his two helpers set up this table and chair. The young man made a table from a few planks of wood and a barrel. The young lady brought out a rough wooden chair. Naberius thought it very quaint that both the girl and boy mumbled, trying to hide their Irish accents. Such was the curse of their birthright in this land, full of its prejudices.

With the meeting now begun, the human men, former soldiers all, lined up in front of the table, while half a dozen of the Dark One's Steam Soldiers stood behind Naberius. The controller box rested on the table with little blasts of electricity buzzing and zapping between the rods at the top. The controller rested atop a book detailing its use and how to make the Steam Soldiers function. The first man in line, who had been a captain in the Confederate army, eyed the controller, and his hand occasionally moved toward it. Behind him, the former soldiers, some of them still wearing parts of their uniforms, eyed the Steam Soldiers with the same looks of hunger that soldiers always had when shown bigger, more destructive weapons than their enemies could ever hope to match. It had been the same all throughout history.

"And your men understand," Naberius reiterated for the fourth or fifth time, "That they all must sign. If one man backs out, the deal is void."

"None shall 'back out' as you say, sir," the former captain said.

Naberius loved the sweet musical sound of the accent of the southern United States; it was prim and proper without the nasal drone of the British upper class. Then again, he'd liked that accent at first as well. After a few centuries, this one might begin to grate, too, if people were still speaking English at all.

"Excellent," Naberius said, and turned to draw the contracts out of his satchel, which he had hung over the back of this wonderfully rustic chair.

He loved – no *loved* is not really an appropriate word for demons, let's say he reveled and savored with exquisite delight – the entrepreneurial spirit that permeated this new continent. It made collecting souls so much easier than in the old world. It was the best part about this country where men dreamed bigger, grander dreams. And most of the time those dreams came crashing against the cold hard world. And most of the time, the cold, hard world won. It made men easier to corrupt.

"We'll just get you all to sign these," Naberius said, still rifling through the satchel – the ink and quills were at the bottom – "and you'll be on your way to a second war of liberation."

While his back was still turned, he heard something thump down on the table.

"Now Captain, you have to wait," Naberius said, turning around, "until…" Someone had put a jack o' lantern on the table. It did not currently have a candle in it, which made sense, as it was the middle of the afternoon. "Is this some kind of joke?"

Naberius looked up. His view of the captain had been obstructed by the young man from the tavern, only now the young man wore a positively ancient coat of black wool stripped with orange silk.

"No joke," the young man said. This time he did not mumble nor try to hide his accent in any way. "Well, maybe a little, but it's on you. See, while these men might hate the North, they hate the creatures of darkness even more, and so they were more than willing to give us a hand with this little ambush."

Naberius tried to stand. He could not pull himself out of the chair. He only struggled for a moment until he realized exactly where he was sitting. He saw no point in fighting a helpless battle.

"Who are you?" Naberius asked.

"My name is Halloween Jack," the young man said. "You and yours have done some grievous harm to me and mine. I mean for you to answer for that."

At that, Halloween Jack picked up both the controller and operation manual for the Steam Soldiers and handed them to the captain.

"I have your word as a gentleman?" Halloween Jack asked.

"Indeed, sir," the Captain replied. "I shall use these constructions only to battle demons and other such machines. No man, be he Northern, foreign, or heathen, should have to face such as these. We still fight with honor."

The captain and Halloween Jack shook hands.

"Fare well, then, Captain Jameson," Halloween Jack said. "I should have my business concluded by the time you get done reading that manual. You can fetch your new toys then."

The soldiers left. And as they did, several of them glanced at Naberius and spat on the ground. That's when Naberius understood his mistake. They were not looking at those weapons to use against the northerners; they were looking forward to using them against his fellow demons. He forgot that sometimes humans could be as subtle as any demon.

"Well played, young man," Neberius said. "Now, just tell me what you want. I'll give it to you, and you can let me out of this chair."

"See boyo," Halloween Jack said. "There's a problem with that. You don't have the power to grant what I want, and I can't let you out of the chair."

"Why not?"

"It's not my chair," Halloween Jack said. He turned the chair around to face the tavern. The tavern keeper and his young lady helper were walking down the steps. Only now the tavern keeper was dressed as a priest and the girl was wearing an ancient-looking, familiar coat of brown wool. "It's her chair."

"Hello, Naberius," Moira O'Neil said.

Naberius recognized her now that she was cleaned up and standing straight and tall, with her hair pulled back from her face.

"Good afternoon, Miss O'Neil," Naberius said. "You've grown a bit since the last time I saw you."

"Oh, shut it," Moira said. "You were there the night the Devil's Gate came down. You were there when my grandmother died."

"Yes, I was," Naberius said, and he realized that gloating about that might not be the best course of action at this particular moment.

"Hurt him," Moira said. "Hurt him a lot."

The chair spun around, and Naberius found himself facing Halloween Jack again. Now the young man in the black and orange coat had a stick in his hand, a stick covered in crosses, and if Naberius wasn't mistaken, those crosses were made of iron and silver. This was going be a very bad day. Unless, he could...

"Wait. Everyone wants something. If I can't get you what you want, I know someone who can. Anything. Anything, name it."

So what if there was more than just a bit of truth to the desperation in his voice? Didn't the greatest lies always hold a grain of truth at the center of them?

"Well, you know the old saying?" Jack placed the stick on the table and stepped away. A mischievous smirk curled the edges of his mouth upward.

"There's a lot of old sayings," Naberius replied. Good. Good. Keep him talking. If they kept talking, it might give Naberius time to play them against each other, or at least figure out what they wanted. "Which are you referring to?"

"Ladies first," Jack said. "And the lady said she wants you to hurt."

Halloween Jack took another step back. The smirk widened to a grin, a grin so malicious that it would not have been out of place on a duke or prince of Hell. That this human could hold such an expression, not just on his mouth, but in his eyes as well…well, that terrified Naberius down to his core.

"Well, my parents raised me to be a gentleman. Those would be the same parents that your kind murdered the same night you murdered Moira's grandmother." The grin faded. Halloween Jack's face became still, as hard and cold as the world that crushed dreams. "And a gentleman always obliges a lady."

Halloween Jack took a few more steps away. Naberius craned his neck around to see Moira and the priest still over by the tavern. Waiting was the worst of it, which is why demons were known to be patient. The imagination played tricks. He just wanted to get this over with.

"Strike, stick, strike, with three fingers."

The stick leapt off the table and began to beat Naberius about the head and shoulders. He brought his arms up to fend off the blows as best he could, but the stick bobbed and wove and came at him from all angles.

As the stick commenced its attack, Halloween Jack walked past Naberius. Moments later, the Tavern door closed. The beating continued through the afternoon and into the evening. As the sun was setting in the west, the Captain and some of his soldiers returned. The captain had the controller and he led the Steam Soldiers away. They buzzed and cranked and hissed their way down the road following the soldiers whose souls should have been his.

As dark fell, Halloween Jack returned.

"Please Jack," Naberius said. "I'll give you anything within my power. Just have your stick stop beating me."

"Don't believe you yet," Halloween Jack replied.

He struck a match on the table and used it to light the three candles inside the jack o' lantern. As Halloween Jack walked away again, Naberius couldn't help but look into the flames behind those triangle eyes. And then the three flames were all Naberius could see. Three flames dancing and weaving. This made protecting himself even more difficult. Eventually, as the night wore on Naberius curled into a ball on the chair, covering his head with his arms and suffering the beating of his existence while three candle flames danced before his eyes, even when he squeezed them shut.

Naberius didn't come fully to his senses until several weeks later. He was on one of the ships crowded with demons bound for England, the center of the Dark One's power on earth. He never told a single one of the demons, all of whom, like him, were fleeing from Halloween Jack, that when the sun had risen the next morning he had given over everything he knew about demon activity in the Americas. Most of the demons on board the ship had suffered at the hands of Halloween Jack because of that information. Naberius felt no shame in that. Even now, if he kept his eyes closed too long, he could see those three candle flames dancing in his mind.

* * *

Saleesh, the succubus, waited in the shadows for the time to be just right. Asag would be angry with her, but Asag was angry all the time anyway, wrath being the sin he was tied to most closely. Halloween Jack had the brutish demon wrapped in that nasty coat, blinded by that horrid lantern, and had released the stick feared far and wide across these colonies to beat upon Asag. At that moment, when Halloween Jack had set all his trickeries to work, was when Saleesh set herself to strike.

She shifted her form to that of a young lady in her late teenage years, perfect in her beauty save for the black eye she fashioned to gain the perfect level of sympathy for the rescuing hero. She'd tried this ploy on Jack of the Lantern once, centuries ago, but The Lantern's wife had nagged the romance right out of him years before he ever took up the lantern. Well, this Halloween Jack was a young man, never married, and so would not have the same protection from her charm. She would be praised for taking him and delivering him to the Dark One. He might even reward her with a title, perhaps even granting her command of a legion or two.

Stumbling out of the shadows, Saleesh wept openly.

"Thank you for saving me," she said.

"Ummm," Halloween Jack said in that way most men did when caught off guard by a pretty lady.

Without waiting for any further response, she flung her arms around him. He returned the embrace, albeit with some trepidation, and patted her shoulder.

"It's...um...alright...miss. He won't...uh...hurt you anymore."

"Thank you. Thank you. Thank you."

Saleesh didn't need to be more creative than that. Men were simple creatures and believed pretty much what they wanted to, especially concerning women.

"My hero should get a reward."

Saleesh stood on her toes, leaning up to give Halloween Jack a kiss. Once she kissed him, he would be hers. No mortal man could withstand the will of a succubus once he had received her kiss.

Just before their lips met, someone landed right next to them. Came from somewhere above and plopped down in the snow right next to Saleesh and the man she was seducing. Saleesh tried to kiss Halloween Jack anyway, but a hand interposed itself between the demon's lips and the lips of her prey. Then the hand shoved Saleesh, shoved her hard, and she stumbled back a few steps, tripped over something, and fell into a chair. Her movement caused the chair to fall over into the snow. Saleesh should have been carried out of the chair when she landed, but she remained firmly seated.

Oh, this is not good, Saleesh thought, then said, "Help me up, sir," in her most alluring voice.

"Oh, shut it," a vaguely familiar voice said.

Saleesh looked at the newcomer. It was the girl from the cottage. The one who helped keep the Devil's Gate closed.

Halloween Jack blinked in surprise. "You were right. It was too easy."

"Off you go, Jack," the girl said. "You've got your own playmate. I'm going to get acquainted with this one."

"Right," Halloween Jack said. Then he faced Saleesh, his mouth curled up into an infuriating, self-satisfied smirk. He tugged his forelock. "Good evening, Miss. Pleasure making your acquaintance." And just like that, Halloween Jack turned his back on the most beautiful succubus in all of Hell.

"Just you and me, now, sweetie," the girl said. "And I don't find you nearly as appealing as he does."

She reached under her coat and pulled out her switch, the switch Saleesh had seen used on other demons and dark creatures who decided to try their luck at gaining the artifacts the women used to keep the Devil's gate closed.

"Maybe we could come to an arrangement," Saleesh said. "There must be something that you want, um, er…I'm sorry, I don't recall your name at the moment."

"You don't deserve my name," the young lady replied. "But you can think of me as Halloween Jill."

With that, the girl raised the switch.

"Please, not the face, not my beautiful face," Saleesh said.

"Alright. I won't hit you in the face if you can give me the thing I want most."

"Anything! Name it, and it's yours."

"I want my grandmother back."

Halloween Jill did not wait for a response.

* * *

Nearly a year after meeting the young man who would become Halloween Jack, Father McDermott stood on the pier at Boston Harbor with Jack and Moira. Though some of the demons had taken to referring to her as Halloween Jill, Moira would always be Moira to Father McDermott. On the other hand, Father McDermott had no problem at all thinking of the young man next to him as Halloween Jack.

The last ship manned by the last crew of demons was sailing from Boston back to Europe. Oh, there would be some stragglers, and that's why McDermott was staying behind. Besides, Halloween Jack's true challenge was just beginning. The Dark One had a secure hold on the British Isles. That was a young person's fight, and McDermott had not been a young man in a long, long time.

"So then," Father McDermott said. "You'll be off to Europe now?"

"Yes," Jack said. "Taking the fight to the Devil himself."

"If I'm to stay and finish cleaning things up over here, you'll need someone else to make three people on this quest."

"I thought Moira and I would look in on our cousin, Daniel. You said he lives in Jack of the Lantern's old Smithy?"

"That's right," Father McDermott answered. "Jack's descendants have always lived there as blacksmiths."

"We'll start there, then," Jack said. "With all Moira and I have done here, think of what we'll be able to do once we have all three of Jack of the Lantern's final descendants together."

"Indeed. Give me a moment to imagine."

The little exchange went almost exactly how they'd rehearsed it. After a few moments, they heard a skittering of claws and a flapping of wings from the docks beneath them. Several shadowy shapes flew toward the ship heading toward the horizon.

"Well," Jack said. "With that last thing done, I suppose we'll be on our way."

Moira kissed the aging priest on the check. "Take care of yourself, Father. We'll see you after."

"You, too."

Then he faced the young man who had become as feared and hated by demons as his penultimate grandfather ever had been. "I didn't think much of you when we first met, but I think Saint Peter was right. You are an extraordinary young man, and if we had to place all our hopes on one man, we could do far worse than you."

"Now don't be going on like that, Father. My work hasn't even really gotten started."

"Was it wise to let the demons know that's where you're headed? They are sure to tell the Dark One."

"Oh, yes," Jack said. His right eye squinted a bit and his mouth made that wickedly charming smirk. "I'm counting on it."

Halloween Jack offered his hand to Father McDermott. They shook like old, battle-tested comrades which Father McDermott supposed, in a way, they were.

Jack sat in the ancient chair that had belonged to Jack of the Lantern. Moira stood behind him and gripped the back of the chair.

"Cork, Ireland," she said, and the magical boots that Jack of the Lantern had won from a faerie lord centuries ago carried them from the shores of the new world to greater and grander adventures in the old world.

* * *

John the Blacksmith prepared to be amused by yet another group of demons coming from the Americas who sought an audience with their dark master. This time, a group of gargoyles stalked into the throne room, except these foul creatures did not walk with the fear and terror most others did who came into this room. The gargoyles moved with purpose from the door to a place maybe twenty yards from the Dark One. All six of them bowed at once.

"What news?" the Devil asked. "You appear to have something for me that is not going to displease me overly much. I hope for your sake, you are correct."

"My Lord," the lead gargoyle spoke, his voice sounding as if it traveled through gravel. "We know where Halloween Jack is going to be. He and his cousin, the girl from the cottage, are going to the smithy where that man," the gargoyle pointed to the cage holding John the blacksmith and John bowed, "wronged you. The last three heirs of Jack of the Lantern will be in one place, at the same time."

"No," John the blacksmith said. "Please, Saint Peter, for the kindness I once showed you, protect my family."

The Devil looked at John with a cold and humorless smile. "Pray all you wish, my old friend. It will not save them from my wrath. My revenge after all this time will be allowing you to live, knowing I wiped your line from the face of the earth." The Devil stood from his stolen throne. "Summon the thirteenth legion and arm them with an equal number of Steam Soldiers. Wait until all three are there, and then destroy the smithy and everyone in it."

Demons of all manner and breeds rushed out of the throne room, with Steam Soldiers plodding after them.

Six

Halloween Jack and his cousin Moira looked down the hill at the cottage and smithy.

It had taken them the better part of a week to narrow down the location of where this whole business had started. Father McDermott had a vague idea that it might be somewhere in Connacht, in central-west Ireland. With Jack sitting in the chair, and Moira hopping around in those boots, they traveled about, collecting rumors and stories, all while avoiding the Steam Soldiers that "kept the peace" and "maintained order for the crown." At first, they'd not bothered to hide who they were, but word had already spread far and wide about Halloween Jack. Both Moira and Jack laughed when they caught a little spider-like thing with the head of a jackal trying to poison a village well. It told them the Devil was offering a princedom for any demon who could bring him the head of Halloween Jack. As much as that amused Jack and Moira, they knew they had to cover their tracks a little better, so they started hopping over to Scotland or England to cause trouble with the demons there. Once they even went to France and saved a village from a particularly nasty plague demon.

They finally narrowed down where Jack of the Lantern's old home might be to a place of about a hundred square miles. They'd spent the last two days hopping back and forth over that territory. They found it, or at least they thought they'd found it. It was the only solitary cottage with a functioning smithy they'd seen. They'd found it just as the sun was setting the night before, and rather than come on their cousin at night, they felt it best to approach in the morning.

Just before dawn, they set down in the trees about a quarter mile from the cottage. They had decided that it would be best to land while still under the cover of night so that the demons wouldn't see them land. They'd timed it right so that they reached the tree line just as the sky brightened into a clear, brilliant blue. Even from here, they could hear the *clang, clang, clang* of the hammer ringing on an anvil.

"Gets to work early, doesn't he?" Moira asked.

"Appears so," Jack said.

He looked over the clearing. A stream ran behind the smithy with a small garden next to it. A chicken coop stood about twenty paces from the house with two doghouses, one on either side. In one of the doghouses, a wolfhound lounged on a blanket that spilled out of the rounded doorway.

Something was odd about that. Why would Daniel keep the dogs outside at night in the snow? Jack had been raised in Boston, mostly, and so he didn't fully understand country ways, but he thought even predators and scavengers would seek shelter at night when it grew this cold. Then he saw a puff of steam come out of the doghouse. He edged along the tree line to get a look behind the doghouse.

"Where are you going?" Moira asked.

"Take a look at that." Jack pointed.

He didn't know exactly what he saw, but it looked like an accordion attached to a kettle which was attached to some of those strange electric rods that buzzed on the tops of the boxes that controlled the Steam Soldiers. Every ten seconds or so, right when the *clang* of the blacksmith's hammer echoed across the clearing, the rods underneath the kettle buzzed, the accordion pumped, and a puff of steam came out of the front of the doghouse.

"Clever," Jack said. "Care to wager that the doghouse on the other side has a similar device?"

"No, thank you," Moira said. "I have learned never to take a bet with you, Mr. Halloween Jack."

Jack couldn't help but smile. While she wouldn't bet with him, he had learned not to riddle with her. Her mind was sharp, and quick to think around corners.

"We should probably say hello," Jack said.

"Indeed," Moira said.

Jack lifted his lantern, he'd gone with a turnip once they'd reached Ireland, swapping it out once for a gourde just for variety and to make the demons wary of any jack o' lanterns they saw on this side of the Atlantic. Moira slung her chair over her shoulder. They'd rigged together a partial harness for it, and thankfully, it didn't weigh too much. Together they left the cover of the trees and tromped toward the birthplace of their family line.

"To think such a small, unassuming place was the start of so much trouble," Jack said, as they approached. "How much of the old story do you think is true?"

"Well," Moira said. "Jack of the Lantern is a decent liar, but I've heard the tale enough times from him and the demons that came through the cottage that I've pretty much decided that the way our family tells it is pretty much the way it happened."

"Oh," Jack said. "I keep forgetting that you've actually spoken to him."

"You'll speak to him, too," Moira said. "After we've won and the Devil and his kin are back in Hell."

"That's if he's still alive," Jack said.

"What do you mean?" Moira asked.

"Didn't the Devil capture him?" Jack said. "After all this time, would the Dark One kill the man that had caused him so much fear and embarrassment?"

"Did you actually listen to the stories?" Moira went into that tone of voice she took whenever she felt Jack needed educating on the difference between the Americas and the olden country. "Jack is already dead. He died old and tired. The Devil can't kill him, so he's got two choices, let him wander free, or allow him into Hell."

"Not exactly a pair of choices the Devil would relish," Jack said. "So, old Dark One below probably has him caged up where he can keep a close eye on him?"

"Fair bet," Moira said. "And, no, I don't want to wager on it. You're too clever and lucky than any three men have a right to be. So, what are you thinking?"

"Huh?" Jack said. "What do you mean?"

"Your eye is doing that squinting thing it always does when you're about to be clever."

"Really?" Jack said. "I'll have to work on getting better about that."

They came to the edge of the yard, the boundary of the yard and the field beyond indicated by a series of wooden posts less than a foot high. Because of the snow, Jack had not seen them from the tree line. A braid of metal wires stretched between each of the posts. As they approached the fence line, a sign rose up from the snow. Jack squinted at it, but he couldn't read the words.

"What is that?" Jack asked.

"It's Gaelic," Moira replied. "It says, 'Mind the path. Do not stray.' "

"What path?" Jack asked.

As if in answer to his question, Jack heard a strong buzzing sound. A series of wipers cleared the snow from a well-worn cobblestone path. The path led toward the cottage. About twenty feet from the cottage, it split. One branch led to the front door; the other branch wound around behind the cottage.

Jack and Moira looked at each other, at the path, and then back at each other. Jack's right eye closed slightly.

"What are you thinking?" Moira asked.

"With the buzzing sound, along with the strange mechanics here, this reminds me a little of the Steam Soldiers the demons use."

She grabbed his shoulder. "You don't think that…"

"Not at all," Jack said. "Daniel might not have been with us, but I can't imagine anyone from the line of Jack of the Lantern helping the Devil or any of his kin. Too much history and all that. No, I'm thinking that this may be an edge for our side."

"You keep thinking, Jack," Moira said. "As scary as it is sometimes, you just keep thinking."

Together they walked down the path, which was easily wide enough for both of them. Still, due to the sign, both made special care to keep a-way from where the snow began. They passed the house and went straight around back to the smithy.

When the doors to the smithy came into sight, both Jack and Moira stopped short. The doors were barred closed from the outside. Jack blink-ed in surprise. Now, in the stories his parents had told him, Jack of the Lantern had trapped the Devil in his smithy for several weeks, leaving him to hammer out hundreds upon hundreds of horseshoes.

"Do you think?" Jack asked.

"That the Devil fell for it a second time?" Moira asked. "I seriously doubt it."

Jack started for the smithy again. Moira grabbed his shoulder. "Are you sure that's a good idea? Daniel, or whoever barred that door closed, probably had a good reason for it."

"Probably," Jack said, "but I've got to know."

"Even if what's behind the door might be the death of you?"

Jack shrugged.

As he got closer, the *clang* of the hammer on anvil grew louder and louder.

Jack got to the door, lifted the bar, and pulled on the handle. The snow on the ground forced Jack to give it several good, hard tugs before being able to get it open enough to stick his head in. When he did, his mouth fell open.

"What do you see?" Moira asked.

"Daniel has a pet ogre," Jack replied.

At the sound of Jack's voice, the hulking creature that worked a blacksmith's hammer up and down, up and down, *clang, clang, clang,* looked at Jack. It was nearly twice as tall as Jack, and its shoulders seemed as wide as Jack was tall. The thing wore a leather coat, wool trousers, and a battered top hat.

"I am no pet," *clang,* "human worm." The ogre's voice was the rumble of the storm against a mountain. Even speaking in what Jack guessed might be its normal tone, the ogre was quite easily heard over the ringing of hammer on anvil. "I am a prisoner." *Clang.* "And if I could let go of this hammer," *clang*, "I would squash you into soup and slake my thirst on your blood."

"Is that *the* hammer?" Jack asked, partially shouting to be heard over the continuous *clang*.

"I imagine so," Moira said, her voice also raised. *Clang*. "Or we would likely be soup by now."

"What are you making?" Jack asked.

He couldn't see the ogre pounding on anything. There didn't seem to be much in the way of blacksmith tools anywhere, nor could Jack see any metal or ore that a smith might use to craft things. Wires and tubes came away from the anvil and stretched across the room to giant metal cylinders in each corner.

"I make nothing," the ogre rumbled. *Clang*. "I pound and pound for centuries." *Clang*. "Trapped here." *Clang*. "Making nothing." The huge creature timed its sigh between two hammer strikes. John couldn't help but smile. The sigh was a perfectly practiced pathetic gesture. The ogre's shoulders slumped as much as they could while it still worked the hammer, the timing of the action never altered for a moment.

"Do you know where," *clang*, "Daniel McRory is?" Jack asked.

"Not here." *Clang*. "Other than that," *clang*, "don't know."

"Umm…thanks." Jack said, shut the smithy door, and replaced the bar. With the door closed, they could still hear the *clang* of the hammer, but they didn't have to shout over it or pause to be heard. "Well, that was completely productive."

"Indeed." Moira rolled her eyes at his sarcasm. "What are you thinking?"

"Not a thing," Jack lied.

"You're lying, again," Moira said. "You're doing the eye thing," she pointed at his right eye and wiggled her finger at it, "again."

Jack sighed. Now that she'd pointed it out, he could feel it. He did his best to straighten his face. When he failed, Jack shrugged. "Might be something." It was a great deal more than something, but like the plan he and Saint Peter had come up with, Jack couldn't tell Moira, or the whole thing might unravel. "Most likely nothing. I'll let you know if I come up with something."

Moira punched him in the arm. "More likely you'll wait to the last possible moment and then tell me only the details I need to know in order to pull off your little scheme."

"Something like that." Jack looked around. "What now?"

"We could try knocking on the front door," Moira suggested. "Isn't that what people do when they come to call on relatives?"

"I suppose," Jack said, "that's what normal people do. Though I stopped considering myself normal the moment I gave my family's last coin away to a beggar and got called upon to save the world. Moments like that change a man."

"Are you sure your parents never brought you to Ireland?" Moira asked.

"For the thousandth time, no, they never did," Jack said. "And yes, I know you think I must have kissed that blasted Blarney Stone a dozen times or more. Alright, front door it is."

They went back around to the front of the cottage, again being very mindful not to stray off the path.

They climbed the steps to the porch. When they reached the front door, Jack knocked. Seconds later, Jack and Moira stepped back when the little slot that Jack hadn't seen opened in the door about the same level as Jack's belt buckle. A rod of metal, wrapped in wires, extended out a foot or so. The rod had a half-sphere of black glass at the end. The rod swiveled to point at Jack and then at Moira.

The thing buzzed, popped, and buzzed again.

"Who are you?" a tinny sounding voice seemed to come from behind the metal sphere.

"I'm your..." Jack started.

The voice cut him off, "What do you want?" as the rod swiveled back to Jack.

Moira said, "We need to speak to Daniel. Daniel McRory. We're his cousins."

The thing swung back to Moira and seemed to look her up and down.

"Liar," the thing buzzed. "Family is all dead." The rod slid back inside the door, and the little slot closed.

"What now, Mister Clever-and-Cunning?" Moira asked.

Jack gave her an irritated, sidelong glance. He pounded his fist against the door.

"Daniel!" Jack said. "We're your cousins. We're not dead. Open the door!"

"Great plan," Moira said. "I'm sure he really wants to talk to us now."

"You have a better idea?" Jack said.

"Maybe try..." Before she could finish, the floor beneath them began to vibrate.

"The tree line." Moira blurted.

Jack tried to reach out and touch her coat before the boots carried her away, but she was already gone. He went to jump off the porch, but the time it took trying to grab Moira's coat left him on the porch a moment too long. Iron bars slid up from the ground, clanging shut at the top of the porch. A sheet of iron slid up over the door, cutting off that escape route.

Jack sighed as he examined where the bars went into both the top and bottom of the porch. He sighed again as he heard Moira's telltale "*oomph*" as she landed next to the cage that had recently been a porch.

Without looking at her, Jack asked, "Couldn't have waited half a breath longer?"

"If I'd waited half a breath longer," Moira said, "we'd have both been trapped. And now we have a bigger problem."

"What's that?" Jack asked, still examining the cage, trying to figure a way out.

"Them," Moira said. "Just like you planned."

Jack turned around and saw a horde of demons in all shapes and varieties, coming out of the woods. Goblins snarled and hissed. Gremlins growled and snapped. Imps cackled in malicious glee. Behind them, surrounded by dozens upon dozens of Steam Soldiers like an honor guard, Naberius sat upon a nightmarish black stallion that snorted fire and stamped lightning. All these demons looked at Halloween Jack, trapped in a cage, and howled their fury.

"Charge!" Naberius yelled.

Moira looked at Jack. "I really hope getting trapped in that cage was part of your plan."

"Not exactly," Jack said, as he placed his turnip jack o' lantern on the floor of the cage. He put the three candles Saint Peter had given him inside it, struck a match, and lit them. He picked up the lantern and held it out toward the demons. A few in the front began to slow a bit at seeing the lantern. Even more slowed, causing quite a bit of stumbling and tripping, when he pulled the pistol out from under his coat. Demons couldn't die, but they could be hurt. "But I think I can work with it."

"Where did you get that thing?" Moira asked.

"One of the soldiers back in the States," Jack replied. "He lost a bet."

He fired the gun into the air. The retort echoed. All of the demons slowed, even Naberius.

Jack pointed the gun at a one of the cottage's windows. He fired again, shattering the glass.

"Get in there and get me out of this cage." Jack tucked the gun into his belt and pulled out his stick. "I'll stay here and break some heads until then."

Seven

Moira un-slung her chair and set it down before she crawled through the window. She found herself in a smaller version of the cage that trapped Jack outside. She was about to scamper back out, when a sheet of steel slammed shut behind her.

"Well, look at you," a familiar voice said. "All boxed up and delivered to me like a little present."

Moira turned as quickly as she could in the confines of the cage. Saleesh, the succubus she'd beaten senseless months before, stood looking at her. Saleesh's face still showed signs of the beating, red lines from the switch crisscrossed her face. Moira's stomach sank just a moment, and then awe overcame her fear as she took in the clockwork menagerie inside the cottage.

Gears and pulleys clicked and turned and buzzed. Here and there, all over the room, blasts of steam erupted at irregular intervals from vents in pipes that ran over the walls, floor, and ceiling. A half-finished Steam Soldier slouched in the far corner. The north wall held a rack of seven strange looking guns – all of them bigger and bulkier than normal pistols and rifles – with odd accessories. Each of the pistols ended with a crystalline globe that sparkled with some inner light. One of the rifles had a bottle on top filled with some boiling, blue liquid, and a tube connected the bottle to the gun proper. A table in the middle of the room had dozens upon dozens of tools scattered across it – some of which Moira couldn't begin to comprehend what they might be used for. The succubus also lounged on the table, bringing Moira's attention to her captor.

Seeing the succubus killed the chilly fear in the pit of Moira's stomach. A burning anger replaced it with such fervor Moira thought she might break into a sweat from the heat of it despite the cold.

"Where is Daniel?"

"He's right below you," Saleesh said. "I like the thought of keeping him warm and snug in one of his own cages. Isn't that right, sweetie?"

"Yes, mum," said someone just below Moira. Daniel – at least Moira assumed it was Daniel – spoke in that same dreamy, sappy, I'm-so-in-love voice Jack had the first time they'd met this creature.

Moira gritted her teeth and forced her mind to work. She had always thought she was quick-witted, but sometimes her cousin made her feel positively slow. Jack was so quick to adapt to new situations and to think around corners, it was frightening. How could she get out of this? Then she remembered the succubus's words, *not in the face.*

Moira felt her mouth break into a wide, Halloween-Jack-wide, grin.

Saleesh shuddered. "You can't scare me with a silly smile. I've got you trapped."

"You are such an idiot," Moira said. "You think you've got me trapped, that I can't touch you, but you are so wrong."

Moira took off her magic boots – the boots that would do their best to go wherever the owner commanded them.

"What?" Saleesh said. "Going to throw your shoe at me?"

"Something like that," Moira said, then she whispered to the boots, "Two inches behind Saleesh the succubus's nose." The boots twitched in her hand. "Hey Saleesh, you've got something on your face."

Moira let go of the boots. They flew across the room and slammed into Saleesh's face. As the boots pummeled the succubus, Moira wondered if demons ever wished they could die.

With Saleesh occupied, Moira put her face up to the bars and looked down as best she could.

"Daniel. I'm your cousin Moira. I'm here to save you."

"I don't really need saving," Daniel replied. "I like it here, and if I stay in the cage long enough, Mistress Saleesh will reward me with a kiss."

"She's a demon," Moira said. "She's lying. Come up to the bars. You should be able to see the truth of it in my eyes."

As soon as she saw a nose poke out from between the bars, Moira smacked it with the switch. Daniel cried out in pain and stumbled back. Then he cried out in indignation and made several uncouth comments about the she-demon. He made these comments in both English and Gaelic, just to be sure to cover his bases, Moira supposed.

"You better?" Moira asked.

"Maybe not better," Daniel replied, "but I'm within shouting distance of my right mind again. Thank you."

"My pleasure," Moira said. "But if you really want to thank me, how about letting me out of this..." beneath her, she heard a click and the squeal of rusty hinges, "cage."

A young man, who seemed the same age as she and Jack, stood up. His clothes were wrinkled. His brown hair hung down in some places and stuck out at wild angles from his head in others. Moira had visions of him trying to cut it himself. Deep green eyes sparkled behind strange spectacles that had a multitude of lenses at the end of twisted wires.

He had a key in his hand and used it to open the cage door.

Of course he still had the key, Moira thought. Saleesh would revel in the perverse joy of allowing Daniel to keep the means of his freedom knowing he'd never have the desire to use it.

"I have determined," Daniel said, "that I really hate demons."

"Runs in the family," Moira said, as she climbed out of the cage.

Once free, she threw her arms around the cousin she'd never met and embraced him.

When she was ready to let go, she remembered, "You have leave to let go of my coat."

"What?" Daniel muttered.

"Just happy to have one more relative alive," Moira said. "And the show of honest affection will help protect you from her." Moira gestured to Saleesh, who was losing her battle to fend off the boots.

"Seems like she's too busy to bother me anymore," Daniel said.

"I'm going to want my boots back, eventually," Moira said. "Now, we have to save Jack — he's your other cousin — and defeat an army of demons. What do those do?" She waved her switch over at the rack of strange-looking guns. "And how do I use them?"

* * *

Things weren't as bad for Halloween Jack as he'd originally expected. Oh, the situation would eventually turn against him, but for now he was alright.

As soon as Moira climbed through the window, Jack had commanded his coat to trap Naberius and had sent his stick to beat that particular Marquis of Hell senseless. Of course, that was after the stick had chased the nightmare horse off by slapping at the beast's haunches. Wrapped in Jack's coat, Naberius found it impossible to maintain his seat.

Still, that didn't do anything to affect the demons standing at the edge of the yard staring at him. He could imagine them thinking: *There he is, that Halloween Jack all the demons who went to the Americas have been talking about. All I have to do is walk right over there and kill him, and then I get to be a Prince of Hell.*

"I've got it," a stunted creature with orange skin and a mass of bright green hair said. "We can throw snowballs at the lantern. Then it can't blind us."

Well, that would certainly work, Jack thought.

The demons also leapt on that idea. Each of them scooped up two handfuls, or clawfuls in some cases, and did the best they could for probably never having played with snow. Granted, Jack couldn't be sure, but he'd heard something about the life expectancy of a snowball in… Well, it didn't matter. What mattered was that the snowballs would probably put the candles out, and his only other defenses were occupied.

"Coat, come back," Jack said. "Stick, come back."

A moment later, his coat came back together around him, and his stick landed in his right hand.

When the demons stopped making their snowballs, they looked at Jack, and faces went slack when they saw he had his coat and stick again.

But before they could put the lantern out, they'd have to get through the yard, and he was fairly certain, considering the predicament he'd found himself in, that getting through that yard was going to be much easier said than done. Speaking of his predicament, Moira certainly was taking her sweet time about getting him out of this cage.

"Lads!" a massive scorpion demon shouted. "He can't kill us! And he can't fight us all at once! Follow me, and the Dark One will reward us all!"

With that, the scorpion demon started toward Jack – right down the path. Jack did not allow the sinking in his stomach to show on his face.

The other demons followed the scorpion demon's example. Goblins, imps, and all manner of nasty creatures rushed toward the cage. And while the scorpion demon worried Jack more than just a little, he leaned back against the steel plate to watch what happened next.

Some vanished in a puff of white powder as they fell into pit traps. Cages and nets erupted from the ground, trapping others. Jack burst into laughter when a giant springboard sent a group of goblins flying well over and beyond the tree line. Their limbs flailing in the air made it look as if they were trying to maintain their flight. His humor was short-lived because the scorpion demon made it to his cage without problem.

Jack banged his stick on the metal sheet behind him.

"Moira!" Jack yelled.

"Not so big and scary trapped in that little cage, are you?" the demon rumbled.

Jack held up his lantern, but the thing just stood up straight and took its eyes above the top of the cage so the candlelight couldn't shine on it.

"Strike, stick, strike," Jack said, "with four fingers."

The stick flew from Jack's hand and began to beat the scorpion demon. The creature just laughed.

"Thank you," the demon said. "I had an itch."

Jack dodged to the side as the tail struck at him from between the bars. The stinger nearly snagged his shoulder. The demon only missed because it couldn't see him.

"Ha!" the demon said. "I can play this game all morning long, Halloween Jack! How long can you keep moving?"

The stinger struck again. Jack dodged again. He could manage this for a while. He had lots of practice moving quickly to avoid Thomas and other bullies. Granted, that had almost always involved more room than the confines of this cage, but Jack would make do until Moira got the door open. Speaking of which — well actually, thinking of which — where *was* his bloody cousin?

To make matters worse, some of the other demons had managed to make it past the defenses in the yard. Jack had seriously miscalculated the number of demons that they would send against them. He supposed that was sort of an indication that his plan to overshadow Jack of the Lantern was working.

Jack ducked under the stinger again and lifted his jack o' lantern at three red-skinned, four-armed demons as they came at the cage flexing their claws. Three paces away, they blinked several times as the candles took hold of them. Still, they came forward and slashed at him as best they could in their blindness. Jack danced and wove back and forth between the arms, and one of the demons screamed as the stinger punctured its arm.

"Sorry," the scorpion demon said, though its laughter indicated he felt little remorse.

"I like this game," Jack said. "Let's see if I can get you to sting all your friends."

Finally, the steel plate slid down and the door behind it opened. Moira stood there with the strangest pair of pistols Jack had ever seen. They looked like oversized flintlocks, but with glowing glass orbs at the ends of the barrels. Behind her, Jack saw a tall, scrawny young man wearing spectacles with a plethora of lenses of various sizes and colors. He held a massive rifle with a bottle of boiling water on top.

"Jack," Moira said, as she leveled the pistols, "duck."

Jack didn't hesitate for an instant. He dropped.

Two blasts of something that looked like solid light flashed by his head with a double *vworp* sound. The blasts caught two of the four-armed demons full in the chest and carried them off their feet and past the tree line. She shot again and the third one joined them.

"What the…" the scorpion demon started to ask, but stopped when the bars from the cage lowered. Its face came into view, probably hoping that it could skewer Jack on its stinger before the candles in his jack o' lantern blinded it.

"Stick, come back," Jack said.

The scrawny young man lifted his rifle. The contents of the bottle bubbled even more furiously, and a jet of blue-white liquid streamed out, soaking the scorpion demon. A moment later, the liquid solidified into ice, freezing the demon in place.

"Jack," the young man offered his hand, "I'm your cousin, Daniel McRory. Would you like to come in?"

Jack took Daniel's hand and let his cousin help him up. While Daniel helped Jack up, Moira dashed over and reclaimed the chair.

"I'd love to." As he rose, Jack saw that Moira was only wearing stockings on her feet. "Where are your boots?"

"Inside, trying to get somewhere."

When they were all inside and had shut the door, Moira waved one of the pistols toward the other side of the room. Moira's boots were hopping up and down, turning a succubus's face into a ruined mess.

"Isn't that...?"

"Yes," Moira said. "She seduced our cousin and put me in a cage. I think she's getting off light."

"Where are your boots trying to get?"

"Two inches past her face."

"Okay then." Jack shrugged. He turned to Daniel. "Do you have a back door?"

"Other side of the kitchen," Daniel said. "Why? We're safer in here while we fight off the demons."

"I need to talk to the ogre," Jack replied. "You might have to set him free."

Daniel's mouth dropped. "Then how will I get power for my experiments and the defenses?"

"I'll figure something out," Jack said.

"But..." Daniel replied. "But..."

"Don't worry, dear," Moira said. "Somehow, he always seems to figure it out."

In truth, Jack already had an idea.

"Alright," Daniel said, but did not seem in anyway convinced.

Moira commanded her shoes to stop trying to get two inches past Saleesh's nose. She slipped them back on and tossed the succubus into a cage.

Jack led the way through the kitchen and out the back door. None of the demons had made it around back here yet, so the trip from the cottage to the smithy was just a short walk. Jack moved the bar and pulled the smithy door open.

Clang.

"Oh," the ogre said. "You again."

Clang.

"I have a bargain for you," Jack said.

Clang.

"I'm listening," the ogre replied.

Clang.

Jack's face scrunched up in concentration. He needed to be sure of what he wanted. Several *clangs* went by while he thought.

"If I can convince my cousin," *clang*, "to set you free, will you," *clang*, "grant me five favors?"

Clang.

"It's supposed to be three favors," the ogre said.

Clang.

"Sometimes things don't happen in threes," Jack replied. *Clang.* "How long have you been trapped there?"

The ogre seemed to consider this as the hammer rose and fell. "Four favors."

"Done." Jack had actually only wanted four. He had asked for five expecting the ogre to haggle. "Daniel, free the ogre."

Clang.

"But…" Daniel started to argue, but the *vworp* of one of Moira's pistols cut him off. *Clang*, and a demon went flying into a Steam Soldier.

"Free him now!"

"Ogre," *clang*, "you have my leave to let," *clang*, "go of my hammer."

The moment Daniel spoke the words, the ogre threw the hammer to the floor and roared with such force that the smithy shook. Jack felt like his bones were rattling in his skin. Then the ogre charged Daniel.

Jack had expected this, and stepping into the ogre's path, he spoke quickly, "First favor: bring no harm to anyone of the line of Jack of the Lantern."

The ogre skidded to a stop inches away from Halloween Jack.

"Oh, you're a clever one," the ogre said, ruffling Jack's hair. "I think I might like you. I think I know what the next favor is going to be, but name it just the same."

"The second favor: help us beat the demons attacking this morning. We'll discuss the last two when we're done with that."

"Easily done."

A pack of goblins rounded the cottage and rushed at them. The ogre pried one of the doors off the smithy and used it to flatten the goblins into the snowy ground.

Jack lifted his stick and his lantern while his cousins readied their guns. Despite there being more demons than he expected, with the ogre and Daniel's weapons this was going to go even better than Jack had planned.

*   *   *

John the Blacksmith, who had once been Jack of the Lantern, watched the Devil as he sat on his throne in Buckingham Palace.

"You seem rather smug and self-satisfied this morning," John said. "Isn't it a bit premature for a celebration?"

"I'm not celebrating yet," the Devil said. "I'm savoring the anticipation, just as I did all those years I waited for the opportunity to strike back at you. Ironically, the means to that opportunity came at the hands of one of your descendants."

"Really?" Jack said, refusing to be baited. He was, after all, speaking to the Father of All Lies. "You don't say."

"Oh yes," the Devil replied. "William McRory, who was the father of one of your last three descendents, never really believed the old stories, despite the ogre pounding away at the anvil in his smithy. William was the type of man who would only see and believe what was right before his eyes or could be tested by science. William and his son were the geniuses that created the Steam Soldiers, and William had a weakness for pretty ladies. One of my succubae seduced him and his son easily. Once we had control of the Steam Soldiers, I only needed one of the McRories to maintain repairs, so I kept the one who would serve me the longest."

Nothing the Devil said could surprise John anymore. He was, after all, called the Dark One for a reason.

"Past victories don't mean you'll see a victory today," John said.

"Perhaps," the Devil said, "but I sent an entire legion against this Halloween Jack. I'm confident in numbers overcoming that troublemaker, no matter how clever he might be."

John the Blacksmith shrugged and waited.

Not long after that, something fell past the large window looking out into the courtyard, then came a large crash. The Devil leapt out of the throne and rushed to the window. More large objects fell from above with crashes coming from the courtyard.

"Let me guess," John the Blacksmith said, "ruined Steam Soldiers?"

"Shut up, blacksmith," the Devil snarled.

Not long after that, a string of demons, battered, black, blue, and bloodied, stumbled into the throne room. The Devil had returned to the throne and surveyed his minions who had failed him with that telltale twitching eye that filled John with so much joy. Finally, Naberius entered, looking like he had seen the wrong end of a dozen ugly sticks.

"My Lord," Naberius said, sounding for all the world like a schoolboy caught cheating on a test, "we have a problem."

"Aside from your failure?"

"Yes," Naberius said. "Much bigger than that."

* * *

Moira followed Halloween Jack through the field of broken Steam Soldiers and beaten and bloody demons. It was a good thing the battle was over – both her guns and Daniel's had run out of power. In the distance, the *clang, clang, clang*, came from the smithy. While not as strong as the ogre, the scorpion demon would serve as a replacement, so all the guns were charging again. Daniel was busy resetting the traps and defenses around the cottage and smithy. Moira and the ogre, who had introduced himself simply as Mickey once the fighting had ended, walked in Jack's wake as he searched the battlefield.

"Ah, here we are," Jack said, when they came upon Naberius trapped with his leg pinned underneath the Steam Soldier's leg, the one that Mickey had ripped off and thrown at the Marquis to stop him from shouting orders. "Moira, your chair, if you please? Mickey, might I entreat you to pick up the leg? No, it's not one of the remaining favors."

"It's fine," Mickey said. "I've always wanted to see this chair in action."

Moira put the chair down. Mickey lifted the Steam Soldier leg and tossed it over his shoulder. Something about fifty yards away cried in pain as the leg landed with a *thump*. Moira stifled a snicker as Jack pulled Naberius up by the collar and shoved him into the chair.

"Wait," Mickey said. "Can I try something?"

"By all means," Jack said, taking a step back.

The ogre lifted the chair and turned it upside down. When Naberius didn't fall out of the seat, Mickey said, "Oooo, this could be fun," and shook the chair, lightly at first, then with more and more vigor. Had Naberius been mortal, Moira was sure his neck would have snapped with how quickly Mickey whipped him to and fro.

"Neat," Mickey chuckled.

"Oh, that's rich," Jack said. "As much as I'm enjoying this, would you mind holding him still? But leave him upside down, I have a message I need to send to his master."

"Sure," Mickey said, and steadied the chair.

John got up close to Naberius's face and stared right into those goat-like eyes.

"Go tell your master the game has changed," Jack said. "When this whole thing started, Saint Peter wanted me to scare the Devil back into Hell. Well, this morning has shown me that no matter how badly I scare the Devil," Jack swept the stick over the battlefield, "he's going to keep coming after me and mine. I'm going to take a page out of General Sherman's book. I'm done trying to scare the Devil. You tell him I'm coming. Tell him that I know a way to rid the world of him once and for all. I'm going to kill the Devil."

"Wait," Moira said. "You can't do that. It's not how things are done. There's centuries of traditions that we have to abide by."

Jack grinned his telltale grin. "If Saint Peter had wanted things done in the traditional way, he wouldn't have asked an American to do it."

"I'm in," Mickey said.

"You?" Naberius said. "You should be helping us!"

"Why?" Mickey asked. "With you lot running around, I'm not the big bad guy anymore. I killed a lot of things before I got trapped pounding with that hammer. But I've never killed a Devil. That should raise me a bit in ogre standing."

"But..." Moira said.

Jack held up his hand, cutting her off. "No. I'm sick of this." Jack poked Naberius with his stick. "The Americas have their own stories and their own traditions. In these stories, we don't just give bullies their come-uppance, we get rid of them. You tell the Devil that if he doesn't go back to Hell and leave us be, Halloween Jack will be the end of him."

Eight

Two weeks later, and one night before Halloween, Halloween Jack sat back in his chair and sipped his coffee while Moira, Daniel, and Father McDermott discussed Jack's change in the plan. After the demons had left the battlefield, Jack had taken Mickey the ogre aside and asked for the last two favors. Mickey railed against the first and laughed at the second, laughed so hard trees around them shook. When Jack went back to Moira and Daniel, Mickey had already left to complete one of the favors.

Both Moira and Daniel had pestered Jack about those other two favors, but Jack refused to tell them what they were. "I wouldn't want to ruin the surprise," Jack said every time they asked him. The truth was, Jack couldn't trust them to act appropriately if they knew, or not to reveal his plans if they got captured. Thankfully, they seemed to grow tired of that response and so stopped asking him about it. Instead, they'd switched tactics, trying to get Father McDermott to get Jack to change his mind about killing the Devil.

As it was, they sat around a table at an inn discussing the matter.

"I'm not sure I can argue against it," Father McDermott said. "I've yet to hear the full plan." Moira had gone to get the priest, and apparently had been babbling about Jack being more than half mad and wanting to break from the old ways. "Spell it all out for us, Jack."

"Well," Jack said, "my father didn't just tell me stories about Jack of the Lantern and other tales of the olden country. He also collected stories of his new homeland, especially stories of its native savages. He'd tell these to me along with our family history. I figure, if our stories were real, why not those? One of my favorite stories was a tale of the Tomahawk of the Four Winds."

"What's a tomahawk?" Daniel asked.

"It's an axe," Moira said. "Like a hatchet. A warrior's weapon used by the Indian Natives of the Americas. They are made of stone or obsidian."

"How do you know this?" Father McDermott asked.

"Jack of the Lantern would bring me books from the Americas when he came to visit," Moira said. "I really like the ones about the western states and territories. I've never heard of the Tomahawk of the Four Winds."

"It doesn't surprise me much," Jack said. "My father only knew about it because he read it in a journal he'd gotten somewhere in his travels before he met my mother. My father was at the Alamo and knew Davy Crockett."

While Moira's mouth and eyes stretched wide, Daniel and Father McDermott blinked at Jack, the name unfamiliar to them.

"Your father knew Davy Crockett?" Moira asked.

"Briefly," Jack replied. "My father was very young."

"Who was this Davy Crockett?" Daniel asked.

"He was an early explorer and American hero," Moira said. "One of the stories claims he killed a bear when he was only three years old."

"Regular Hercules, this Crockett fellow was," Daniel said.

"Actually, he kind of was," Jack said. "In his journal, Davy Crockett wrote about the Tomahawk of the Four Winds."

"Wait," Moira said. "I thought everyone died at the Alamo. How did your father get out?"

"My father was just a boy, and so he was allowed to leave with the other women and children before the fighting began in earnest. Now, let me tell the story of the Tomahawk of the Four Winds."

Jack took a drink of his coffee, cleared his throat, and began.

"Long before the white man came from the great waters to the east, the People lived in harmony with all the spirits of the land. Some spirits were tricksters and sometimes played jokes on the People and their fellow spirits, but there were no spirits of evil in the land. This was not always so. Long ago, when the spirit world and world of men were closer than they are now, evil spirits crossed back and forth between both worlds, causing pain, strife, and suffering everywhere they went. The spirits went to the Great Spirit and the men went to their chiefs, asking for someone to deliver them from these embodiments of evil. The Great Spirit came to the land and visited the greatest of all the chiefs. The Great Spirit told this chief how he could rid the worlds of these terrible spirits. To make the story short, the greatest chief had many adventures making the Tomahawk. He found a special stone that fell from the sky and took it to the four corners of the land and had it blessed by each of the four winds. The greatest of all the chiefs took that tomahawk and used it to kill all the evil spirits so that the People and the spirits could live in harmony."

Jack paused to let the story sink in.

"I'm going to get the Tomahawk of the Four Winds and use it to kill the Devil."

"But you don't know if it's even real," Daniel said. "And even if it is, you don't know where it is."

69

"It is real. And you're right, I don't know where it is, but I bet I know how to find out where it is." Jack grinned at Moira. "Any takers?"

"Saints in heaven preserve us," Moira said, and buried her head under her arms on the tables.

"Gents?" Jack said. "Either of you?"

"Not on your life or mine, Jack my boy," Father McDermott crossed himself. He'd lost nearly as many wagers against Jack as Moira had in their campaign to rid America from the demons.

"How can you two be sure?" Daniel asked.

"Did he ask you to bet on it?" Moira asked, her voice muddled underneath her arms.

Daniel nodded.

"Then he's figured out some way to win the wager," Father McDermott answered. "He might not win in any way you expected, but he'll win. For example," the priest turned to Jack, "you know where the journal is."

"As a matter of fact," Jack said, "I believe I do. You see, Davy Crockett gave the journal to my father so that the Spaniards couldn't find it and learn all of his secrets."

"Of course he did," Moira said, lifting her head. "And you know where the journal might just be, don't you."

"As a matter of fact," Jack grinned even wider, "I believe I do."

All three of them jumped when Mickey the ogre put his face up to the window next to them and said, "Then let's go get the bloody thing and kill us a Devil. Oh, and I got those things you asked for, Jackie boy."

As they caught their breath, Mickey handed Jack a satchel.

"What is that?" Father McDermott and Moira asked at the same time.

"Father McDermott, Mickey the ogre. Mickey, Father." Father McDermott gaped at Mickey.

"Charmed," Mickey said. When the priest wouldn't stop gaping, Mickey looked at Jack. "What's with him?"

Jack shrugged. "I have no idea. I told him about you."

"I'm terribly sorry," Father McDermott said. "It's just that you're, so...so..."

"Ogre-like?" Mickey asked.

"That's it!" The Father exclaimed, and then flushed. "I'm terribly sorry."

"Ah, yes," Mickey said. "No offense taken, Father. I get that a lot."

"So, Jack," Moira said. "Bag. What's in it?"

Jack smiled at Moira. "It's a surprise. Like everything else, you'll get to know at the right time."

Moira glared at Jack, and he hated that he couldn't tell her everything, but again, he couldn't risk letting any part of the plan get out into the open or the whole thing might come crashing down around them.

"Bu...bu...but..." Father McDermott stammered. "An ogre?"

"Yeah," Jack said. "He's on our side. At least until I get one more favor out of him."

"How many has he done for you already?" the priest asked.

"Three," Jack said.

"And he's still owes you one more?" the Father said. "Besides, he can't go with you, that will throw off the number."

"Oh, he's coming," Jack said, "and so are you, because?"

All at once, Moira, Daniel, and Mickey said, "Sometimes things don't happen in threes."

"Right," Jack said, and swallowed the last of his coffee. "Now that we've gotten that out of the way, let's go get that journal."

He stood from the table, and halfway to the door he paused to make sure his cousins and the Father were following him. They were, though none of them looked pleased. In fact, each of them looked as if questioning his sanity, which was, of course, part of the plan. Jack wanted the demons to see that his friends also thought he was more than a little crazy. Hopefully, that would add to the mystique Jack was creating around himself. From the window, Mickey winked.

People watched as Halloween Jack walked through the inn. Jack wondered how he must look, wearing the strange orange and black coat, carrying his stick and jack o' lantern, a pumpkin now that he was back in the United States. And even if his own appearance wasn't enough to cause a stir, he had a menagerie of strange companions following behind him: a priest, a girl with a coat similar to his with a chair slung over her shoulder, and the tall scrawny fellow with the spectacles with all those strange lenses and the weirdest gun they'd ever seen. Jack grinned widely and nodded at whoever looked at him, which made each and every one of them quickly look away.

This was to be his lot in life. He and Saint Peter had spoken of it at length that night that felt like a lifetime ago. He needed to be larger than Jack of the Lantern had ever been, in the minds of the Dark One and all his kin, as well in the minds of his fellow men.

Halloween Jack stopped in the center of the inn. Still grinning, he swept his gaze over the entire room.

"Good evening, ladies and gentleman," Jack said. "All Hallow's Eve is coming, and it's going to be a darker night than usual this year. All manner of foul beasties are roaming free." He placed his jack o' lantern on a table and lit the candles inside it. Once all three candles were burning brightly, Jack spun his lantern, sending shadows wavering and dancing across the inn. "Don't fear the darkest beastie of them all. I'll have him well and taken care of, you just make sure that you have your jack o' lanterns out to frighten off those that follow him."

"Are you saying that you're Jack of the Lantern?" someone asked from across the inn, from somewhere behind him. "Because you haven't been doing a very good job the last few years."

Jack didn't bother turning. "Not at all. Jack of the Lantern was my grandfather, and he retired. I've taken up things in his place. My name is Halloween Jack, and I'm going to have a little chat with the Dark One himself and set some things straight on how things are going to be."

"And if the Dark One doesn't like what you tell him?" someone else asked.

A few people laughed at that. Jack let his face go blank and swept his gaze over the room again with no grin, no frown, no expression whatsoever.

"Then I'll kill him. I'm Halloween Jack, and I have the means to do so."

With that, Jack picked up his lantern and left. Hushed conversations had already sprung up all throughout the tavern. When he stepped off the steps leading up to the inn's door, Jack saw a coach driving by. He grinned and tugged on his forelock as it passed by.

A moment later, Father McDermott caught up to Jack. "Well, that wasn't very subtle."

"It all depends on your outlook, Father," Jack replied. "It all depends."

His cousins fell into step with them.

"You're a mad man," Daniel said.

"More than a little," Jack replied. "But the world needs it, and I've been told I'm the only one that can do the job."

They rounded the corner of the inn. Mickey was waiting for them in the shadows, and the shadows did quite a good job of hiding the huge creature.

"I don't understand," Father McDermott said. "Shouldn't it be helping the Devil?"

"First off," Mickey said, "I'm a *he* not an *it*. Second, not in the least. I am a living creature. I hadn't even been born yet when that war in heaven thing happened. Don't care about their politics. I happen to like the world just the way it is, or was. I may be wicked and mean at times, but not inherently *evil*. Besides, we ogres, trolls, giants, and other such folk pride ourselves on getting one over on others, the bigger, more self-righteous, and pompous the person we get one over on, the better. Why do you think there are so many stories of us beating up on knights? Getting one over on the Devil himself sounds like a lot of fun." Mickey looked at Jack. "Do you think they went for it?"

"I'm pretty sure," Jack said.

"What do you mean?" Moira asked.

"Oh, there were at least three demons in the common room back there," Mickey said. "Because, sometimes, things do happen in threes."

Moira glared at Jack. "Did you know they were there?" When Jack nodded, she added, "What game are you playing at, John O'Brien?"

"Moira dear," Jack said. "There is no John O'Brien anymore. There can't be. I must be, for the sake of the world, now and for as long as I wander, Halloween Jack. If I allow myself to be anything but him, they will win, because then I will be only a mortal man. They have no need to fear a man, only a legend, and I've only got a short time left to solidify this legend. I don't have the luxury of the lifetime that Jack of the Lantern had. My legend must be total and complete, and it must be now. The surest way to solidify that legend is do something no one else has done. Killing the Devil should do the trick.

"Now, my old home isn't far away. Shall we go see if we can find Davy Crockett's journal?"

Without waiting for a response, Halloween Jack headed into the night. Oddly, Mickey the ogre was the first to catch up to him.

* * *

Naberius hung upside down, chained to the ceiling of the carriage. The Dark Lord had seemed to enjoy this torment ever since Naberius had told him about the events at the cottage and smithy of Jack of the Lantern. As the carriage rolled past Halloween Jack, the man had tugged his forelock. Had he known who was in the carriage? He couldn't possibly know, but he seemed to be able to know other things, and his wits were quicker than any being Naberius had ever known.

"I told you," Naberius said. "And now, thanks to the ogre, we know how he plans to do it."

"You did indeed," the Dark Lord said. "But all things considered, I needed to verify this for myself. Once this young man started making trouble, I should have taken matters into my own hands, rather than leave the details to my lessers."

Naberius did not comment that the Dark Lord had dealt personally with Jack of the Lantern, and that hadn't worked out very well for all of demonkind.

"Do you think the ogre can be trusted?" Naberius said.

"Of course not," the Dark Lord replied. "It's an ogre. It will do whatever serves its own best interests at any moment, but we can trust that it is not truly Halloween Jack's creature, either."

Naberius wondered at that. Halloween Jack made it a habit to cover all his bases, and even the things that appeared to be left to chance always seemed to work out in his favor. The Marquis of Hell couldn't help but respect and even admire the young human, especially with that cocky tug of his forelock. Oh yes, Naberius decided, Halloween Jack knew exactly who was riding in the carriage, and that simple gesture had been a challenge. As with Jack of the Lantern, the Dark Lord did not realize what he was up against. Well, Naberius knew, and hanging from the ceiling in his chains, he decided he was finished being a Marquis of Hell. He wanted a bigger title, and if Halloween Jack managed to kill the Dark Lord, someone would need to fill the role of Lord of Hell.

"What are you smiling about?" the Dark Lord asked.

"I'm looking forward to seeing the expression on Halloween Jack's face when you best him," Naberius replied. He silently thanked the Dark Lord for teaching all his followers to lie so well.

Nine

Halloween Jack stood in the street flanked by his friends, looking at the mansion that had been the childhood home of John O'Brien.

"You actually grew up there?" Moira asked.

"It's bigger than I remember," Jack said.

Jack looked at the house, trying to reconcile his memories with the reality of what he was seeing. Until this moment, he wasn't sure the plan was going to work, that Saint Peter would actually be able to grant his second wish, but the proof stood in front of him. More to the point, twin sets of memories warred in his mind: what John O'Brien remembered about growing up and what Halloween Jack remembered about growing up as John O'Brien. Two men with two pasts, sharing the same body. Halloween Jack supposed it would be enough to drive a lesser man mad, while he just took it in stride as part of what needed doing.

"The house looks a bit out of place," Daniel said.

And the house did. The house was actually a large mansion surrounded by modest family homes.

Halloween Jack sifted through his conflicting memories. "Our house is older than the neighborhood, built before the O'Brien family came to America. My grandfather used most of what was left of the family treasure to buy it. The neighborhood sprang up around it as Boston grew."

"You also have another problem," Mickey said, and pointed to a light flickering in a window on the second floor.

"Lord, why can't anything be easy?" Moira asked.

"We're up against all the forces of darkness at the same time," Father McDermott said.

"If it were easy," Jack added, "it wouldn't be worth doing, and it wouldn't be nearly so much fun."

"*Fun*, he says," Daniel said. "Jack, boyo, you have a strange definition for that word."

"Have you met him?" Moira asked.

"Children," Father McDermott interjected. "This banter is not helping. Jack, where is the journal?"

"It's probably in my Father's study on the second floor," Jack replied. "One room over from where that light is. Moira, get me up there. Daniel, Father, make sure none of them get past you going down the stairs. Mickey, stay out here and demolish any Steam Soldiers that might show up."

"Happily," Mickey rumbled.

Jack placed his jack o' lantern in his right hand and gripped Moira's shoulder with his left. He'd come to notice the slight tingle as the magic of the coat bound his hand to it.

"Boots," Moira said, "take me to that window over there."

Jack's stomach lurched as they flew into the air, him being pulled along by the combined magic of Moira's boots and coat.

About halfway to the window, Jack said, "Strike, stick, strike, with four fingers."

His stick flew from the pocket in his coat and slammed into the window, shattering it.

"Stick, come back," Jack called, and the stick slid back into its pocket inside the coat.

A moment later, he and Moira landed in the room amidst the shattered glass. Two Steam Soldiers flanked the door. A pack of goblins stood at rough attention against the far wall. A finely dressed man sat in the high-backed chair behind the massive desk in the center of the room. The man had slick black hair, a thin mustache, and a pointed beard. He wore a scarlet tailcoat over a midnight-black waistcoat. His eyes held a mischievous twinkle, and a knowing smirk played across his lips. Naberius hung from chains, dangling from the ceiling, just behind the Devil's left shoulder. Two more Steam Soldiers puffed and buzzed behind the Marquis of Hell.

"It's a pleasure to make your acquaintance, at last," the Devil said, as he flipped through a battered journal that seemed to have seen dozens of miles for each year it had been carried about the early American frontier.

"This is so not good," Moira said. "Halloween Jack, you've my leave to let go of my coat."

Jack pulled his hand free. "Naw. This is going to be fun."

"You really need to reexamine how you define that word," Moira muttered under her breath.

"Please, Jack," the Devil said, "let's not be hasty. Just because I didn't get along with Jack of the Lantern doesn't mean we can't come to some sort of agreement."

"So you'll go back to Hell, and only come out once a year, setting things back to the way they should be?" Jack asked. "Done. We'll meet you and yours by the Devil's Gate and be done with this nonsense."

The Devil laughed a deep amused laughed, the sound of it soaked with sweetness and honey. Jack so wanted to like the man who made that laugh.

NO! Jack yelled within his mind. *He is not a man. He is the one that commanded his demons to murder your entire family, hundreds throughout Europe and America, who bore no other guilt than being born into the wrong family.*

"I don't think so, Jack," the Devil said. "Aside from the trouble you've been causing, my kind like it very much on this side of the Gate."

"Well I suppose, then, might I make another offer?" Jack asked.

"I'm listening," the Devil said.

And that was the moment Halloween Jack truly knew, deep in his bones, that he would win. It was the same reason that Jack of the Lantern had won. The first Jack must have realized the Devil's weakness, just as Halloween Jack had recognized it now. The Devil couldn't resist the chance to bargain. Also, he must not be able to take anything from someone that wasn't freely given, otherwise he wouldn't need the Steam Soldiers or the other demons to hunt and kill for him. He would just strike down his enemies as soon as they became a nuisance.

Jack grinned his widest, maddest grin and directed it at the Devil. The Dark One's knowing smile faltered and the mischievous twinkle in his eyes faded.

"Strike, stick, strike," Jack said, pointing at Naberius, "with two fingers."

Naberius might appear to be trapped in those chains, but Jack didn't trust any appearances around those two.

As the stick flew from its pocket, Jack tossed the jack o' lantern at the Devil. Instinctively, the Devil dropped the journal and caught the pumpkin. The moment he did his eyes glassed over and three candle flames danced in the reflection.

The goblins scurried forward. Moira already had her pistols out and was shooting away. *Vworp, vworp, vworp!* Blasts of yellow light carried the goblins backward, slamming them into the wall as they slid to the floor. They did not get back up.

The Steam Soldiers by the doors started forward. The ones standing behind the Devil raised their arms. Jack remembered all too well what that meant.

"Mickey!" Jack yelled. "Steam Soldiers up here!"

Jack didn't wait for any kind of response. He sprang for the desk and the journal. His hand closed around the book. Before he could pull his arm back, Naberius grabbed Jack's wrist. Jack tried to pull against the Marquis's grip, but could not. For all his cunning and wit, Halloween Jack was only human and could not match the strength of the demon lord. Even as Jack's stick beat Naberius, he locked eyes with Jack and smiled.

This was not part of the plan.

Behind him, Jack heard Moira's guns *vworp*ing, goblins screaming and groaning, and Steam Soldiers clanking, hissing, and buzzing.

"I have the human boy, My Lord," Naberius said. "Please give me this one chance to redeem myself. You know where this savage weapon is, go and claim it for yourself. I will hold your enemies here."

With that, Naberius knocked the jack o' lantern away from his master with his free hand. The pumpkin sailed across the room and shattered against some curtains. The three candles fell to the floor, still burning, unable to go out on their own. The curtains caught fire almost immediately.

"I'm used to the flames," Naberius said, eyes sparkling. "I actually quite like them. Can you say the same? Shall we remain here and find out?"

"Thank you, Naberius," the Devil said. "It was a pleasure to meet you, Jack, just this once before you die."

The Devil vanished. Heat washed up from the room.

This was not part of the plan.

A crash came from the window where Jack and Moira had entered the room, not breaking glass, but snapping wood. Jack glanced back. Mickey had ripped his way through the window and charged one of the Steam Soldiers. The ogre picked it up and used it to pummel one of the others to scrap.

Jack looked back at Naberius, who was still grinning at Jack. Jack struggled against the grip. This was definitely *not* part of the plan.

"Stick, strike with four fingers," Jack said.

Naberius grunted with each blow, but he did not release Jack's wrist.

"You think your little stick will dissuade my ambition?" Naberius asked. "When all I have to do is hold on a little while and suffer a bit of discomfort before your stick burns to cinders, and after your bones do the same the Dark Lord will make me a Prince of Hell. No, I will not let go because your stick is beating me." And then Naberius released his grip on Jack's wrist.

"Stick, come back," Jack said. The stick returned to Jack as he backed away from Naberius. All Jack could wonder was, "Why?"

"Something about being better to reign somewhere or other," Naberius said, and vanished from the room.

Jack was too busy snatching up the journal to stop Naberius from escaping; likewise, Moira and Mickey were too busy with the goblins and Steam Soldiers.

By the time Moira and Mickey had destroyed the Steam Soldiers and the goblins had run off — at least those that were still conscious had — the fire had spread across half the room.

Jack stood watching the flames get closer and closer, bigger and bigger, trying figure out how to get his three candles back.

"Jack," Moira yelled. "We have to go."

"My candles," Jack said. "I need them."

"They's gone, Jack," Mickey said.

"No," Jack said. "They can't burn up. Once they melt all the way, they will grow back. It's part of the blessing from Saint Peter."

"Then let's wait for the house to burn down, and we'll get them after," Moira said.

"No time," Jack now had to yell over the flames. The heat forced him back to the door with his cousin and the ogre. "The Devil knows where the Tomahawk is. We've got to get there before him."

Behind them, footsteps echoed in the stairwell. All three turned: Moira raised her pistols, Jack got ready to command his stick, and Mickey picked up a Steam Soldier's severed arm. It turned out to be Daniel and Father McDermott.

"What are you doing," Father McDermott cried. "We've got to get out of here?"

"Jack won't leave without his candles," Moira said. "They won't burn up, but they're trapped in the fire. Jack's trying to figure out how to get them."

"You really need those candles?" Daniel asked. When Jack nodded, Daniel shook his head and pushed his way past them. "Well, this will be the end of this gun until I can get it back to the smithy and recharged."

Daniel sprayed the freezing gun all over the room. Steam and smoke filled the air, but within moments, the flames were out. The bottle at the top of the gun was empty.

They waited a few minutes for the smoke and steam to dissipate. Daniel adjusted his spectacles and found the candles in no time at all. He held them out to Jack, but when Jack reached for the candles, Daniel pulled them away.

"What?" Jack said. "Give them to me? I need them for the plan."

"Halloween Jack, how can someone as smart as you be such a bloody idiot sometimes? You don't have to do everything yourself, every single time."

"I'm Halloween Jack. I'm the one Saint Peter chose to follow in the footsteps of Jack of the Lantern. He did everything pretty much by himself."

"And look where that got him," Daniel said.

"Not to mention my grandmother," Moira said, "and the rest of our family."

Jack stood in the ruins of his father's study, looking at his candles in Daniel's hand. Slowly, he faced each of the people in the room, Daniel first, Moira, Father McDermott, and then Mickey.

Mickey shrugged. "You do what ya gotta do, Jackie Boy."

"Alright," Jack said. "Saint Anthony's church isn't far from here. We'll talk there, where the demons can't overhear us. Now, may I please have the candles?"

"Yes," Daniel said. "Now that you're done being an idiot."

"At least for now," Moira said, and punched Jack in the shoulder.

* * *

A little over an hour later, Jack sat drinking tea and coffee with Moira, Daniel, and Father McDermott in a back room at Saint Anthony's church. Father McDermott had impressed upon one of the priests there that they needed succor. Mickey was outside, patrolling, making sure that they were not interrupted or overheard. Unlike at the inn or back at the smithy, Jack did not want the demons to overhear this particular bit of conversation. It didn't take him long to go over the plan. In theory, it was fairly simple. In execution, a bit more complicated. And, as much as he hated himself for holding back, Jack kept the important details to himself. If they knew what he truly planned, it wouldn't work.

"So you really worked all this out the night you met Saint Peter, Moira, and myself?" Father McDermott asked. "Why didn't you start with trying to kill the Devil straight away?"

"It wouldn't have worked," Jack said. "Even though I knew about the Tomahawk, I couldn't have just said, 'Hey, I'm off to kill the Devil.' We had to work to create the legend of Halloween Jack into something that they believed was capable of that."

"But still," Daniel said, "you had this plotted every step of the way?"

"Most of it," Jack said. "I didn't plan on Mickey. He was a crazy random happenstance that I took advantage of, but I knew about your inventions, Daniel, and thought I could use the smithy as a place to strike more fear into the demons. I didn't know about you being a prisoner."

"Lucky you had me along," Moira said.

"Lucky indeed," Jack replied. "All along the way, things have not gone completely according to my grand design, and each time someone was there to help recover from that. Thank you, all."

Jack took the satchel that Mickey had given him at the inn and handed it to Moira.

"What's in this?" Moira asked.

"The other six things you need to perform the ritual to close the Devil's Gate," Jack replied. "That was my third favor from Mickey. I figured even if he couldn't get them, it was worth a shot, and as it turns out, he could, which saves us a lot of time and effort."

"What was the forth favor?" Daniel answered.

"I can't tell you," Jack said. "It's something that has to stay between Mickey and me." He saw the questioning expressions on their faces, and it broke his heart that he couldn't share that part of his plan. "Please trust me?"

They looked back and forth at each other. Surprisingly, Father McDermott was the first to speak.

"Alright, John," the priest said. "You're the one that's had this thing going since that first night. I'll trust you. I didn't think much of you when we first met, but you are exactly what Saint Peter said you'd be. What do you need from us now?"

"Thanks for the confidence, Father," Jack said. "Captain Jameson and his squad of soldiers, along with the Steam Soldiers we gave them, should be at the smithy soon."

"You must have sent them there right after we first beat up Naberius," Father McDermott said.

"I did," Jack said. "I honestly thought they would get a bit of rest, as we'd be chasing down the things Moira needed. Thanks to Mickey, we don't need to worry about that anymore.

"Moira, after you take me to the Alamo, get Daniel back to his smithy so he can arm the soldiers and take them to the cottage. You'll need someone to protect you from the demons trying to stop you from repairing and closing the Devil's Gate."

"How will you get there?" Moira asked.

"That's where Mickey's final favor comes in," Jack replied. "I'll be there at the exact right time."

"What should I do?" Father McDermott asked.

"Pray for us," Jack said. "We're going to need any edge we can get. And, you'll need to take up the fight if we fail. I thought this was a sure thing when I planned it, but as we've seen, sometimes things don't go according to the plan."

"Well," Father McDermott shook Jack's hand, "God's speed son."

"Thank you, Father," Jack said, "for everything."

They left Saint Anthony's and met up with Mickey.

"Alright then," Mickey said. "We ready to go and get this axe and go kill the Devil, himself?"

Everyone nodded. Jack and Mickey each put a hand on Moira's coat. As always, Jack felt that tingling as his hand became fixed to it.

"The Alamo," Moira said, and Boston fell away underneath them.

Ten

Jack had never been to Texas, but he was fairly certain that there wasn't supposed to be snow on the ground the night before All Hallow's Eve. It was a still night. In the distance, the Alamo was just a dark shadow against the moonlit sky. They had put down just a ways away from the fort in case the Devil had put out sentries.

"So, this is Texas," Mickey said. "I thought it would be bigger."

Jack punched him in the arm.

"What?" Mickey asked, but when Jack glared at him, the ogre broke into a wide grin. "Sorry, couldn't resist."

"I don't get it," Moira said.

"Don't worry about it," Jack replied. "It's not actually that funny."

"If you say so," Moira said. "Are you sure you can get to the cottage without me?"

"We'll be there," Mickey said.

Moira eyed the ogre. "Alright."

She threw her arms around Jack and squeezed him. Jack held her back, and in doing so, realized he was scared. Terrified. Rather than just hold Moira, Jack squeezed back, squeezed back as if it were the last embrace he'd ever feel. In a way, it might as well be.

"You alright?" Moira whispered.

"Just scared," Jack said. "I've got a lot riding on my shoulders. I just hope I'm strong enough to do what needs doing."

Moira tried to pull away from Jack but couldn't for a moment, the magic of her coat holding them together.

"You've my leave to let go of my cloak," Moira said.

All three of them had a short laugh over that, then Moira grabbed Jack by the shoulders.

"Not that I've known many men, but my heart tells me you're among the strongest in all the world. You've defied the Devil to his face and somehow managed to scare him and the denizens of Hell in a shorter time than Jack of the Lantern. I know you haven't told us everything, and that's alright. It's the way you do things. I believe in you. I know you'll do whatever needs doing. After all, you're Halloween Jack. Now go fetch that bloody tomahawk so we can end this nonsense." She ruffled his hair. "Saint Anthony's church in Boston."

Moira vanished into the night sky.

Mickey stepped next to Jack. "Scared, eh?"

"Wouldn't you be?" Jack asked.

"I suppose," Mickey said. "How much did you tell them back at the church?" the ogre asked.

"Pretty much nothing," Jack replied. "They think they know the plan, or at least most of it, when really, they don't know much of anything."

"They're going to hate you for it when they find out."

Jack shrugged. "Maybe. Maybe not. You'd be surprised how understanding humans can be once they see the larger picture."

"How much do I know?" Mickey asked.

"More than they do," Jack replied, "but not all of it."

"It's not too late to change your mind on that favor."

"It's the best way to get done what needs doing," Jack said.

Mickey ruffled Jack's hair. "You're a good man, John O'Brien."

"What did I say about that?" Jack said.

"Pssshhh. That silly rubbish about being one or the other? I'd been a-round a long time before I got trapped pounding on that blasted hammer, and I knew all manner of men. Knights, farmers, princes, rogues, and a host of others. Some I got along with, others I fought with, even killed a few of them. Don't look at me like that, Jackie Boy. I'm an ogre, it's part of what we do. Anyway, the point is: no man is ever just one thing, and this *Halloween Jack* thing you've made yourself out to be wouldn't likely go through with what you have planned. That's the choice of a man, not a legend. That's what the Devil and his kin fear more than anything. That underneath all that Halloween Jack has become, there is still a man, desperate to save the world and avenge the ones he loves."

Jack punched Mickey in the shoulder. "Thanks. You're a good friend."

"Been a while since any man has called me a friend," Mickey said, then ruffled Jack's hair. "Now, let's go get that bloody tomahawk so we can end this nonsense."

"I'm all for that," Jack said.

Jack struck a match and lit the three candles in his jack o' lantern. He used the light to examine the journal and find out the location of the entrance to the secret chamber where Davy Crockett had hidden the Tomahawk of the Four Winds.

"The Devil knows it's here," Jack said. "The journal states that plainly. Let's just hope he couldn't decipher the code to tell exactly where it was before we interrupted him."

"What's the code?" Mickey asked.

"The directions are spelled out by reading every seventh letter of every third page," Jack said, flipping through the journal. "Got it. We need to get around to the chapel. Crockett held the wall near there. We'll have to dig through about a foot of dirt to get to the hatch leading down to the chamber below."

"That sounds like a lot of work to do in short amount of time," Mickey said. "You sure that's accurate?"

"Don't underestimate the power of determined and desperate men," Jack replied.

Mickey nodded. "You would know."

They crept to the fort. Several times they hid from patrols of demons and Steam Soldiers. Jack was amazed that such a large creature as Mickey was able to hide so well. It took them longer than Jack would have liked, but eventually they crouched against the outer wall. Only a few feet of stone separated them from the chapel. They could hear the Devil shouting inside the fort.

"I don't want excuses," the Dark One said. "I want that weapon found before Halloween Jack arrives. I will name whoever finds it Prince of the Americas once we conquer the world."

"Prince of the Americas," Mickey muttered, tapping his chin thoughtfully. "Quite a title. I wonder if that applies only to demons."

"Oh, you're funny," Jack said. "And looks aren't everything."

"That hurts me, Jack," Mickey said. "Hurts me to the bone."

"I'm sure," Jack said. "Now we need to figure out how to get in there without the Devil and his kin seeing us. Oh, and get the Tomahawk of the Four Winds and get out without them discovering us."

"Easily done," Mickey said.

He lifted Jack onto his shoulder and scaled the wall. Just below the edge, Mickey paused while a pair of Steam Soldiers and an imp patrolled by. They scrambled over the edge of the wall and crouched together on the chapel's roof.

"Now how do we get in?" Jack whispered.

Mickey pried up a section the roof large enough for them to drop down.

"How's that?" the ogre asked, and tossed the rubble to the far side of the Alamo.

"What was that?" something yelled with a voice like grinding metal.

The plaza of the Alamo filled with shouts and sounds of scurrying demons and Steam Soldiers.

"No!" The Devil's voice rang out over the din. "Don't send everyone. It might be a diversion."

"Crafty one, that Dark One is," Mickey said.

"Not too crafty for us, though," Jack replied.

He read the journal and counted out the steps from each wall to where the hatch to the secret chamber was hidden. Three steps from the altar and seven steps in from the wall.

"Would you mind?" Jack asked, gesturing to the spot he'd marked out.

"Can't you do anything yourself?" Mickey asked as he began scooping up dirt and rock as if his hands were giant shovels.

"What do you mean?" Jack said. "I came up with this plan. I'm the mastermind that's going to save the world."

"Well, I suppose." Mickey cleared the last of the earth from the wooden hatch. It turned out to be about a yard down. Three feet. That figured. "I'm just glad I'm not you after you climb out of that hole."

"I don't blame you," Jack said.

"It's not too late, Jackie Boy," Mickey said. The honest concern in his eyes touched Jack to the point he felt tears welling in his eyes. "You're a smart lad. Almost as smart as me. If we beat our heads together a bit, we could probably come up with another plan."

"Beating our heads together would only wind up with me unconscious."

"I didn't mean literally," Mickey said, "you silly git."

"I know." Jack shook his head and sighed. "It's got to be this way. It's the only way I'll be able to keep them in line for as long as that line will need to be kept."

"Alright then," Mickey said, and pulled the hatch up. A ladder led down into the darkness. "I'll see you in a few minutes."

Jack nodded, tucked his pumpkin jack o' lantern under his arm, and started climbing down.

The ladder had twenty-one rungs, just as Jack had thought there would be. A tunnel led off into darkness. He followed it for twenty-one paces. Again, just as he had expected. A door waited at the end of the tunnel. Jack placed his hand on the latch. Even though he knew the weapon beyond this door had been waiting for him, butterflies still danced in Jack's stomach. He was alone for the first time since that night when Saint Peter, Father McDermott, and Moira had told him of his birthright. No one was here for him to posture in front of. No one to see the façade of Halloween Jack that hung over John O'Brien. Jack and John stood in that tunnel alone with each other and the realization of what was coming. John and Jack cried for a good long while.

After the tears stopped, Halloween Jack opened the door.

The Tomahawk of the Four Winds lay on a stone pedestal. The head was a piece of carved obsidian just about as big as Mickey's hand. The haft wasn't wood, but the bone of some giant creature, and was as long as Jack's arm. And that was it. Jack had expected a bit more. Perhaps some feathers, or other ornamentation. Something, anything, more. But the weapon was just the head and the haft.

Jack looked at it for a moment, considering this ancient weapon that served no other purpose than to wait here for him to take it and save the world. He wondered if Mickey might be right. Was there some other way? Jack sighed. There might have been back when this whole thing started, but not now. He couldn't go back and change things. The irony of that thought made Jack snicker. No, he'd set events in motion to lead him to this path. As his father, his real father, had said time and time again in the tiny townhouse where John O'Brien had really grown up, *You're far too clever for your own good, John, and one day it'll be the death of you.* Well, Halloween Jack had turned out to be far more clever and far more foolish than John O'Brien had ever been.

Jack picked up the Tomahawk of the Four Winds. It wasn't as heavy as he thought it was going to be. As light as the wind, he supposed.

He hefted the weapon onto his shoulder, leaned against the wall, and waited. If he made it seem too easy, they might not buy it. With that thought, he took some dirt from the tunnel floor and smeared it over his face. He also struck himself in the forehead with his stick until he felt a trickle of blood run down his face.

"There," Jack said to himself. "Now I look like I've just retrieved a weapon that will kill the Devil."

* * *

A while later – it was hard to judge the passage of time in the darkness of that cave – Jack climbed up the ladder. The moment his head came into the chapel, a massive hand grabbed the back of his neck, and another covered his mouth before he could order his coat and stick to attack.

"Terribly sorry, Jackie Boy," Mickey said, "but it seems that princedom was open for anyone, and I just really like the sound of Mickey, Prince of the Americas."

Jack struggled against Mickey's grip, even tried biting the ogre's hand, but the ogre just chuckled.

"Excellent," the Devil said from just outside the chapel door. "I had a feeling it might be in here. No wonder we couldn't find it."

"Drop the axe, Jack," Mickey said. "Or I'll snap your neck like a twig."

Jack dropped the Tomahawk of the Four Winds. Mickey kicked it out the door. The Devil picked the weapon up and looked it over.

"I was expecting something more," the Dark One said, then shrugged. "It matters not. I have it, and I'll use it to crush the last hope your world has to escape me."

"I'm going to let you go, Jack," Mickey said. "Don't do anything stupid."

Mickey released Jack.

"Strike—"

Before he could speak the second word, Mickey slapped him. The blow sent Jack flying out of the chapel. Black spots danced across his vision, and his jaw hurt so much that he couldn't even begin to think about speaking.

Demons crowded around Jack, kicking and pummeling him. Jack curled into a ball, covering his head with his arms, trying his best to go someplace else to ignore the pain.

"Stop!" the Devil yelled. The beating stopped. "I understand your zealousness to repay him, but I don't want him killed...yet. Now someone get his things."

The demons all moved away from Jack.

"Oh, you bunch of babies," Mickey said.

Jack felt the ogre lift him off the ground and strip him of his coat and stick. Jack had dropped the jack o' lantern when the ogre had hit him. Jack tried to say something again, but every time he tried to move his mouth, pain shot through his head.

"Broke your jaw, Jack," Mickey said. "I told you not to do anything stupid."

Mickey put the coat and stick into a rough sack. The sack looked like it already had the jack o' lantern in it.

Mickey faced the Devil and held out the bag. "You don't mind if I hold onto these?" Mickey asked. "I want to show them off as trophies to the other ogres."

"By all means," the Devil said. "It's not like anyone else can use them. Please, bring him along."

Mickey grabbed Jack by a foot and dragged him up some stairs to overlook the courtyard of the Alamo. All the demons gathered below cheered at the sight of him beaten and defeated.

The Dark One addressed his kin. "Look at this wretch, this puny thing who has tried to take the place of Jack of the Lantern. I have defeated him in less than a fraction of the time it took to defeat The Lantern. The line of Jack of the Lantern holds no power over us! Remember, my children, every creature has a price. All we must do is be patient and victory will eventually be ours. Now that we have broken them, let us lay claim to this world!"

The demons cheered again.

"Prince Mickey of the Americas," the Devil said.

"My Lord," Mickey bowed.

"Would you kindly fetch the priest and meet us at the cottage?" the Devil asked. "I believe you know the way."

"As you command, My Lord," Mickey said. He waved the bag above Jack. "See you soon."

Mickey left, taking the bag with Halloween Jack's three treasures with him.

The Devil himself loomed over a battered and broken Halloween Jack. "I've won." He held the Tomahawk of the Four Winds out above Jack. "You've no coat, no stick, no lantern, and no weapon to use to kill me. All that you have fought for will soon be lost."

The Devil's laughter echoed across the plaza. The world shifted, and a moment later, that laughter echoed across the plain that held a simple cottage and the path leading to the Devil's Gate.

The plain was a mess with the ruined husks of Steam Soldiers littered everywhere. All around the cottage, demons groaned, unable to die, no matter how many injuries they suffered from the defenders. Jack recognized some of the soldiers and Captain Jameson. They'd turned the cottage into a fort. A mound of dirt had been erected around the cottage with sharpened stakes protruding from the dirt.

"Just a few more moments boys," Captain Jameson yelled, waving Daniel's ice gun. He stood on the roof between two of the Steam Soldiers.

The former Confederate soldiers had made some additions to the Steam Soldiers that Jack had given them. The two remaining Steam Soldiers had been fitted with a carriage in back that housed a pair of Gatling guns pointing over the shoulders. A host of about a hundred demons charged the cottage. One of the Gatling guns roared, spraying bullets into the assault. Moments later, those demons still capable of moving retreated.

A flight of gargoyles dove toward the cottage. A cannon sort of thing popped up next to the Captain. Daniel sat behind the weapon and fired a massive net made of metal. The net caught all but two of the gargoyles. Jack noticed a long wire connected the net to the cannon-like thing Daniel was operating. Daniel pulled on a crank at the top of the cannon. Electricity flashed through the wire and net. Gargoyles screamed as they fell to the earth. When the electricity stopped, the gargoyles lay twitching on the ground.

A great groaning of metal echoed across the plain, and all fighting stopped.

The great metal gates that had once kept the Devil's Gate closed, barring Hell from the Earth, rose and reattached themselves to become the Gates of Hell once more.

"Good girl," Jack said. Pain lanced through his head from his broken jaw, but it was worth it.

"It's a shame she's too late," the Devil said, and then shouted "Stop! I have both Halloween Jack and the Tomahawk of the Four Winds! Throw down your arms, and I will spare him."

Jack really hoped they would ignore the Devil and keep fighting. They didn't. In only a few minutes, all Jack's friends were standing in front of him, surrounded by all the hordes and legions of Hell. Mickey had arrived with Father McDermott. Jack wasn't really surprised that they had all stopped fighting; they didn't realize the Devil's weakness.

"We've stopped fighting," Moira said. "Let him go."

The Devil chuckled. "That was not the agreement. I only said I wouldn't harm him."

"Excuse me, My Lord," Mickey said.

"Yes?" the Devil said.

"You only promised that *you* wouldn't harm him."

"That is correct."

"Would you allow me a small bit of retribution for years of tedious servitude?"

"Absolutely," the Devil said. "Use this." The Dark One handed Mickey the Tomahawk of the Four Winds. "I will enjoy the irony of it."

"So will I," Mickey said. The ogre cocked his arm back. "Good-bye, Jack. Say hello to Saint Peter."

Jack closed his eyes. Even though he'd known this was coming, still, he didn't want to see it coming.

A moment later, the Tomahawk of the Four Winds slammed into Halloween Jack's head. His skull caved in. He heard Moira scream. Jack had barely enough time to think, *Oh Lord, that hurt*, before he died.

Eleven

"Please, no," said the soldier standing in front of Halloween Jack. "We died fighting to give you time."

Jack blinked a few times. A soothing light surrounded him. A line of people stretched out in front of him. The group of men directly before him wore the uniform of Confederate soldiers. Jack felt smaller than he had in all his life.

"Sorry, my friends," Jack said. "I had to die sometime. Everyone does. Don't worry. Saint Peter is going to be glad to see me. It's all part of the plan. I'll be sure to tell your friends you went to a decent place."

Jack left the line as two more people appeared behind him. He sprinted toward the giant pearl-gold gates in the distance.

The line was longer than Jack expected, though he didn't know why or what his basis for any kind of comparison was. As he ran down the line, he heard shouts from other people who were very unhappy to see him here. Jack ignored them. He had to get back, and only one person could send him there.

Just as he expected, he saw Saint Peter looking over his book and chatting with the person at the front of the line. Saint Peter still had the same serene look of patience about him, but the glow he emitted the last time Jack had seen him was absorbed by the permeating holy light of Heaven.

Jack waved at Saint Peter and cut to the front of the line, jostling an old lady out of the way.

"Excuse me," Jack said, lifting his hand and smiling guiltily, "but I'm kind of in a hurry, and you've got all eternity ahead of you. You understand, right?"

The lady blinked a few times in surprise. "Well, I, uh…"

"Thanks so much." Jack turned to Saint Peter, blinked himself, then turned back to the lady. She looked twenty years younger than she had a few moments before. "You're French? And you're speaking French. How can I understand you?"

"This is Heaven, Jack," Saint Peter said. "That's one of the tiniest miracles we can work here."

"You're that Halloween Jack fellow," the French lady said.

"I am," Jack said. "Would love to chat more, but can't."

And Jack would have loved to chat with her for as long as she liked. She had continued to grow younger and younger, until she seemed about Jack's age. She had dark hair, and even darker eyes – deep brown that invited him to sink into and drown in them. She smiled at him sweetly, and said, "A shame you have to run off. You seem wild and fun." Her voice was the warm kiss of a summer's breeze.

"You don't know the half of it," Jack said, and though it broke his heart, he turned his back on the French beauty. "I'm here." Jack said. "Can I come in?"

"I'm sorry, Jack." Saint Peter flipped through his book. He reached a page and read it over. "You can't. I've been keeping an eye on you. You've stolen jack o' lantern after jack o' lantern and used them to house candles blessed with the magic of Heaven. Not only that, you've lied again and again to kith and kin. You've even attempted a bargain with the Devil himself. Since you died without confessing your sin, if I let you in they might clip my wings."

Jack grinned. "I had a feeling you might say that. I suppose it's the torments of Hell for me."

"I *might* be able to get you time in Purgatory," Saint Peter said.

"Naw," Jack said. "I'd rather the torments of the Dark One's realm than the tedium of all that waiting."

"Well...if that's how you want it," Saint Peter said.

"Yeah. That's how I want it." Jack's grin grew even bigger and wider. It felt so good to do that without hurting. "Better send me to the Devil's Gate so I can ask to come in."

Saint Peter looked Jack over. His expression had changed from serene to curious.

"What?" Jack asked.

"A long, long time ago, I remember having a similar conversation with a relative of yours. However, he came here, shocked that he wasn't getting into Heaven even though he'd done me a kindness. He didn't realize that he'd unwittingly barred himself from gaining entrance to paradise. It was only by happenstance that he became the symbol humanity uses to protect itself on the darkest night. And now here you are, knowing that you're being kept out of Heaven on mere technicalities. You've fought the good fight to your death, and now you're going to fight it even more."

Jack nodded. "Someone has to do it. Didn't you say I was the best suited?"

"I did at that."

"Then why are we still discussing this? I've got a world to save."

"Good-bye, Jack," Saint Peter offered Halloween Jack his hand. "You're a good man."

Jack shrugged, reached out, and shook hands with a Saint. "Sometimes I have my moments. I'm ready."

"Not yet," the French, now young, lady, said. She stepped next to Jack, stood on her tiptoes, and kissed his cheek.

"What was that for?" Jack asked.

"You came to my town and saved it from a demon trying to spread a plague. You saved my grandchildren." Then she kissed him on the mouth.

A blush crept from his cheeks to his ears. For what seemed like the first time in his life, Halloween Jack did not have a retort prepared.

"Alright," Jack said after he caught his breath. "*Now*, I'm ready."

A moment later, Jack was lying on his back. He could hear Moira crying to his right. To his left, the Devil was ranting about something. Jack didn't bother to pay attention to what he was saying. The Devil paused, and all his minions and followers cheered. Jack had been waiting for that.

Halloween Jack sat up. The cheers died.

"Excuse me?" Jack said. "Might I get into Hell? It seems I've nowhere else to go."

The hordes and legions of Hell screamed as one. The Devil spun and sputtered in his surprise. Off to his side, Jack's friends and family knelt, guarded by demons and Steam Soldiers. Mickey was closest of all and still held the Tomahawk of the Four Winds.

Jack grinned.

"Oh, but first, coat, trap Mickey."

The bag tucked into Mickey's belt writhed and jerked with such force that it came free before Mickey could grab it. The sack fell to the ground, opening up. Jack's coat flew out of Mickey's sack and wrapped around the ogre.

"Stick, come back," Jack said.

The stick leapt out of the sack and flew into Jack's hand as he stood up.

Mickey struggled against the coat. Jack stepped up to the ogre, and gripping the stick with all four fingers, he slammed the stick against Mickey's wrist. The ogre cried out, and dropped the weapon.

"That was for my jaw," Jack shouted. Then Jack snatched up the Tomahawk of the Four Winds.

"Stop him," the Devil screamed. "Someone, stop him!"

"And this," Jack said, raising the Tomahawk of the Four Winds, and for once, not even the faintest hint of a smile "is for killing me." Jack leaned over and gently tapped Mickey lightly on the forehead with the Tomahawk.

The ogre screamed. His body went tense. He twitched once, twice, and thrice. His eyes rolled back in his head, and with a great gurgling sound, Mickey the ogre dropped to the ground. His chest neither rose nor fell.

"Coat, come back."

The ancient-styled black coat, with its orange silk sashes, came apart, releasing the unmoving ogre. The pieces of it flew through the air and came back together around Jack.

Halloween Jack turned to face all the hordes and legions of Hell. In one hand, he held his terrible ever-striking stick, in the other, he held the Tomahawk of the Four Winds. He grinned his widest, craziest grin and beckoned all those demons with his two weapons. He imagined a pair of dark eyes looking down on him from paradise and puffed up in his chest.

"Yes!" Jack yelled. "Someone stop me! Step right up. I bet you could all get me in a rush, but I promise, I'm going to go down fighting. Oh, yeah, and it's not like you can kill me again."

Jack took a single step forward.

Each and every demon took a step back.

Jack turned back to the Devil. The Devil glanced from Jack to Mickey's prone form.

"You knew the ogre was going to betray you," the Devil said.

"I had an idea that he was," Jack replied. "He was an ogre after all. If not him, you'd have gotten one of them to do it for you." Jack waved the Tomahawk of the Four Winds at the armies of Hell. "I arranged it so that I wasn't going to get into Heaven."

"Clever," the Devil said. "I thought killing you would get you out of my hair. People who actively fight me usually get a ticket to the front of the line."

"Too bad I'm a liar and a thief," Jack said. "Those two details kind of killed that plan, huh?"

"Right you are. I notice that you haven't used that thing on me." The Devil gestured to the Tomahawk of the Four Winds.

"No, I haven't. I will, if I have to, but I've got this dilemma in killing you. You're the evil that I know. I have plans of how to deal with you in charge of all of them." Again, Jack waved the ancient weapon at the assembled demons. "If I kill you, someone else is going to take your place. I have no idea what that is going to look like. I know that he," Jack waved his stick over at Naberius, "let me go, hoping I'd kill you so he could fill the void left by your absence."

Naberius let out a tiny *meep* when the Devil turned to stare at him.

"Don't act so surprised," Jack said. "You rule over demons."

"I'm not surprised in the least." The Devil turned back to Jack. "What do you propose?"

"Easy," Jack said. "I want things to go back to the way they were before. You and yours go back to your side of the Devil's Gate. Moira and her descendants will keep the Gate closed every night of the year except All Hallow's Eve. I'll be wandering about with my lantern." To emphasize this, Jack wandered over to Mickey's bag, pulled out the pumpkin, and lit the candles that were still inside. "I've got three candles; I might get an apprentice or two. Point is, you never know which of those lanterns will be me or mine."

The Dark One sighed. "Then I and all my kin will surely take care when we see them. I agree to these terms. Do we have an accord?"

"Not quite yet," Jack said. "Any members of my family who happen to find themselves in your care that you killed the night you broke loose must be freed to Purgatory."

"Fine," the Devil said. "I don't really relish the thought of watching over them for all eternity, worrying about when they are going to start trouble."

"And, Jack of the Lantern. You must free him into my custody."

"Fine," the Devil said. "He's not nearly so much fun now that he's lost his legendary status to you. But on this point you must actually give me something in return."

"Oh, this should be rich," Jack said. "What?"

"You have a scorpion demon bound in service to the hammer. He is a good and loyal servant – well, as loyal as a demon can be. I want him back. That one can take his place." The Devil waved at Naberius. "He no longer pleases me."

"But...but..." Naberius blubbered. "Please—"

"Oh, shut up," the Devil said, and waved his hand absently at Naberius. The Marquis's mouth vanished.

"Neat trick," Jack said.

"Unfortunately it only works on demons," the Devil replied. "I can think of a few others I'd like to be able to do that to."

Jack grinned.

"We go back to Hell and only venture forth again on the Darkest Night, unless of course, someone neglects the Ritual of Closing for an evening. Your relatives go to Purgatory. And I free Jack the blacksmith and give you Naberius, Marquis of Hell, in exchange for one semi-loyal scorpion demon."

"Sounds about right. Do we have an accord?"

"We do." The Devil offered his hand to Halloween Jack.

"Are you kidding?" Jack asked, and eyed the hand as if it were a serpent.

"One must try," the Devil said.

Jack rolled his eyes. "Yes, as long as I don't have to touch you, we have an accord."

"Excellent," the Devil said.

Naberius vanished. In his place stood the scorpion demon that had tried to kill Jack, and a portly, balding, middle-age man.

"Alright everyone," the Devil called, "we're going home!"

Many of the demons groaned, but despite their disappointment they began to file away through the Devil's Gate.

"Well played, Halloween Jack," the Devil said, "well played. I truly look forward to our next game."

"I'll be here whenever you want a lesson in clever and cunning," Jack said. "I'm not getting any older, anymore. Just know that next time, I won't be so nice."

Several of the demons in the Dark One's honor guard shuddered when Jack said that. Jack grinned at them and saluted with the Tomahawk of the Four Winds.

Now freed from their captors, Jack's friends rushed over to him. Moira reached him first. She hit him. Jack blinked in pain, and by the time he recovered Moira had her arms around him. After a few moments, she let him go. Jack came away from her embrace easily.

"Your coat?" Jack asked.

"In the cottage," Moira said. "I had to take it off for the ritual."

"You're a bastard, Jack," Daniel said. "I understand why you didn't tell us about the dying part, but you're a bastard."

"And that's why you wouldn't ever join me for confession," Father McDermott said.

"All part of the plan," Jack said. "Your reaction to me getting killed had to be real enough to convince the second greatest liar there is." He offered his hand to Captain Jameson. "Thanks for helping, Captain."

"It's Alistair," the retired officer said in that distinct accent of the Southern States. "That's what my friends call me."

Jack turned and watched as the Hordes and Legions of Hell filed back through the Devil's Gate.

"Enjoy this sight," Jack said. "God willing, no one will ever see it again."

After a few moments, Moira said, "They're far enough away, Mickey, you can get up."

The ogre sat up and took in a great gasp of air. "It's about bloody time."

Twelve

Halloween Jack sat back in his chair, drinking his tea, and smiling his first natural smile since the night he'd assumed the role of humanity's protector on the Darkest Night. The trophy of their victory, the Tomahawk of the Four Winds, lay in the center of the table. Moira, Daniel, and Father McDermott also sat around Moira's table. Mickey leaned against the back wall — he'd climbed over the walls and come in through the roof which hadn't been there since the morning the Devil's Gate came down. The soldiers were outside, cleaning weapons and tending to the wounded. John the blacksmith, who had once been Jack of the Lantern, stared out the back window at the Devil's Gate.

"When did you figure it out?" Daniel asked.

Everyone had calmed down since the ogre's "resurrection." Jack thought he would probably chuckle for at least a decade the way Father McDermott and some of the soldiers had shrieked. In fact, he laughed right then.

"What?" Father McDermott asked.

"Nothing," Jack replied, and went back to drinking his tea.

Truthfully, that had been the only amusing part. The rest of Jack's friends were ready to kill the ogre. If Moira hadn't been on Jack's side, they probably would have tried. Moira was the one who suggested tea while they let Jack explain.

"I should have realized earlier," Moira said, "but watching Mickey split Jack's skull traumatized me beyond rational thought. I started putting pieces together when Jack sat up. I remembered the first favor Jack asked Mickey, 'Bring no harm to anyone of the line of Jack of the Lantern.' So the fourth favor must have been to counteract the first, but only for Jack specifically."

"So even if the Tomahawk didn't kill Mickey," Daniel said, "why didn't you use it on the Devil and be done with it?"

"Because the Tomahawk doesn't actually do anything," Jack said. "It's just an elaborate prop."

"What?" everyone asked at once, even Mickey.

"Well, at first I wanted Saint Peter to make me a weapon that I could use to kill the Devil. Saint Peter told me that he couldn't actually create that kind of weapon, even with a heavenly wish. It took some explaining that I didn't want a weapon that could do it. I just wanted a weapon with a story to make people think it could. So Saint Peter went and put everything into place so that we could chase after the Tomahawk of the Four Winds. That's why the house seemed so out of place in that neighborhood. It's also why it had to be a weapon and story native to the Americas. I got the idea that night when the imp that was trying to kill me with the Steam Soldiers said something about them still trying to figure things out on this new continent. They wouldn't have time to verify the truth of the story.

"Mickey was the perfect straight man for me. Being an ogre, the Devil assumed that Mickey would betray me in hopes for a title and other rewards."

"I still like the sound of Mickey, Prince of the Americas," the ogre said.

"You would," Moira said. "Why didn't you betray Jack?"

"I had agreed to do him four favors. One of which I hadn't taken care of at that point. Besides, I'm fond of the world just the way it is. Don't like demons. Can't trust them. Now, don't say a word. I've been a good companion."

"That you have," Moira said.

"Here, here," Daniel added. "A finer companion we couldn't ask for, even if you did kill our cousin."

"A sham," Father McDermott said, staring at the Tomahawk. "You gambled the fate of the world on a sham."

"Not entirely," Jack said. "I actually had to die without confessing some pretty nasty sins – and no, I don't want to go into the details – so that when I did die, I couldn't get into Heaven. Saint Peter sent me to the Devil's Gate so I could ask to get into Hell. I had to become more terrible than Jack of the Lantern, which meant I had to be eternal, just like he was, otherwise, they could just wait me out."

"Now what?" Daniel asked.

"We wait," Jack said. "He's going to try again. He can't help himself. When he comes, I'll be waiting for whatever he pulls."

"What about us?" Moira asked.

"Well, you guys, too," Jack said. "If you're still around."

"What do you mean?" Daniel asked.

John the Blacksmith cleared his throat. "How long did it take the Devil to get the better of me? And I'm not nearly as clever and cunning as Halloween Jack is. Basically though, the Devil is patient, and he knows one of Halloween Jack's advantages is that he has all of you. He'll probably wait until Jack is alone to strike again."

Silence fell around the table as they all sipped their tea.

"I suppose that's it for me then," John the Blacksmith said. "I should be heading to my new home."

"New home?" Moira asked.

"I'm not the feared Jack of the Lantern anymore," John said. "There's nothing keeping me out of Hell, where I was supposed to go in the first place."

"About that," Jack said. "Saint Peter, I'd like to cash in my third wish now."

A few moments later, perhaps a total of three moments later, someone knocked on the door. Moira hopped up from her chair and opened it. Saint Peter stood there in all of his saintly radiance.

"Might I come in?" Saint Peter asked.

"Absolutely," Moira said. "May I get you some tea?"

"No, thank you," Saint Peter said as he entered. "You've taken over a year for this, Jack. What would you like?"

"I wish for John the Blacksmith, formerly known as Jack of the Lantern, to be forgiven his trespasses as is only right for the centuries he has walked the earth, alone and lonely, so that he could protect humanity from the Devil and his kin on the Darkest Night."

John the Blacksmith's mouth moved up and down, trying to form words. Finally, he managed, "You're using your last wish to grant me passage to Heaven?"

"That I am, Grandfather of mine," Halloween Jack said. "You've suffered enough torment and loneliness." Jack turned to Saint Peter. "Is that alright, or are we going to argue over this wish, too?"

"Granted," Saint Peter said, "with no arguments. Shall we go John?"

"Thank you," John said to Halloween Jack.

"It's the least I could do," Jack said. "I'm not going to send my grandfather into the clutches of the Dark One if I have a way to stop it, and I do."

Moira got up and embraced John.

"I won't be able to bring you books anymore," John said.

"I think I can live with that," Moira said, tears rolling down her cheeks.

"I can get the books," Jack said. "Now off you go, before I change my mind."

"You cannot change your wish once is it made," Saint Peter said. "Good-bye, Halloween Jack."

In a flash of light, Saint Peter and John the Blacksmith were gone.

"Where will you go, Jack?" Moira asked.

"I'll wander," Jack replied. "It's part of the job. I'll be back by once a year or so, around the end of October."

"You get lonely," Daniel said, "you know where the smithy is."

Jack nodded. "I might stop in from time to time."

Halloween Jack pushed his chair away from the table, put his mug down, and picked up the Tomahawk of the Four Winds. He shook hands with Daniel and Father McDermott.

Moira pulled off her boots. "Halloween Jack, I give you these boots as a member of my bloodline." She handed them to him. "These will speed you back to us when you get too lonely."

"Thank you, cousin," Jack said, and slid them on. "But you keep the coat and chair. You might need them."

He pulled her into his arms and held her tight.

"I'll miss you," Jack said.

"No you won't," Moira replied. "You'll find some kind of trouble to distract you before too long."

Jack shrugged, "Maybe. But it isn't going to be the same without you."

And with nothing left to say, Jack left through the cottage's back door. Alistair Jameson was waiting for him. The Captain saluted Jack as he came out.

"You, sir, are one crafty fellow," Alistair said. "I'm glad we're on the same side. I wanted to let you know the boys and I are going to stick around, keep an eye on things here and at the smithy. And to be honest, I think a few of the men have taken a shine to Miss Moira."

"You make sure they treat her like the lady she is," Jack said, "or they'll answer to me."

"They'll answer to both of us," Alistair said.

They shook hands, and Jack continued on toward the Devil's Gate.

After seven paces – Jack rolled his eyes at that – Mickey fell into step beside him.

"Really?" Jack asked.

Mickey laughed the deep rumbling laugh of an ogre. "I couldn't resist."

Jack lengthened his stride a bit, while Mickey shortened his.

"Don't you think you've stirred up enough trouble for one day?" The ogre asked.

"Not even by half," Jack said. "I need him to know how thoroughly I got him."

"Normally, I'd warn against it," Mickey said, "but in this case, I think you're right. Especially since he's not going to come to the gate himself."

"That's unlikely," Jack agreed.

They walked together in quiet until they reached the massive gates to Hell. Jack rapped the haft of the Tomahawk of Four Winds against the gate, and for a moment he thought he saw a horseshoe embedded in the iron of the gate. Jack shook his head and waited. A slot opened in the door, two beady red eyes looked out, and immediately the imp started blubbering.

"Relax," Jack said. "I'm not going to do anything. I just want your master to have this."

Jack handed the imp the Tomahawk of the Four Winds and walked away.

"He's going to be mad," Mickey said.

"Most likely," Jack replied.

They passed the cottage, and when they came to the edge of that place that lies between all places, a great and furious roar echoed out from inside the walls of Hell so that the Devil's Gate rattled and shook.

"Yeah," Jack said. "I'd say he's pretty angry."

Again, Mickey laughed his deep, rumbling ogre laugh as they continued walking.

After a few hours, Mickey asked. "What's Heaven like? I'll never go there. Nor will I go to Hell. When my kind dies, we just fade from the world, but it would be nice to know what Heaven is like."

"Heaven is…" And that's the point when Jack realized he couldn't recall much about Heaven. He knew he'd spoken to some people, and a pair of dark eyes flashed in his mind, a pair of eyes that invited him to dive in and drown. "I know what Heaven was for me, but it would be hard to explain. I think Heaven is different for everyone."

"Fair enough. Mind if I tag along?"

"Not at all. Don't have any plans until the Devil stirs up trouble again. You?"

"None that I can think of. I'm happy just to not be beating on that anvil anymore."

They walked for a time in silence, then Mickey said, "We could see if any other holidays need shaking up. If you want?"

M Todd Gallowglas has been a professional storyteller at Renaissance Faires and medieval festivals for roughly twenty years. After receiving his Bachelor of Arts in Creative Writing from San Francisco State University in 2009, he used his storytelling show as a platform to launch his fiction career through the wonder of the eBook revolution. His *Tears of Rage* sequence, as well as *Knight of the Living Dead*, and *Halloween Jack and the Devil's Gate* sneak onto several Amazon bestseller lists every so often. His short story "The Half-Faced Man" received an honorable mention in the Writers of the Future Contest. He is a regular fiction contributor for the Fantasy Flight Games. With it all, he's still trying to wrap his head around his success and is trying to find the perfect balance between writing, gaming, and airsoft battles (because it's not as messy as paintball) on the weekends.

M Todd Gallowglas is a proud member of the Genre Underground.

Made in the USA
Las Vegas, NV
10 September 2021